THE
AKO CAINE PRIZE
FOR AFRICAN
WRITING 2020
SHORTLIST

The AKO Caine Prize for African Writing 2020

First published in 2020 in Europe and Australasia by
New Internationalist Publications
The Old Music Hall
106-108 Cowley Road
Oxford
OX4 1JE, UK
newint.org

Cover illustration: Ricardo Gomez Angel/Unsplash

Design by New Internationalist

Printed by TJ International Ltd, Cornwall, UK, who hold
environmental accreditation ISO 14001.

MIX
Paper from
responsible sources
FSC® C013056

British Library Cataloguing-in-Publication Data
A catalogue record for this book is available from the British
Library.

ISBN 978-1-78026-579-7

Foreword

The stories shortlisted for this year's AKO Caine Prize for African Writing bear witness to the phenomenal talent and diversity of African writers. In a year when so much in everyday life has taken on the quality of the extraordinary, and so much has been disrupted, the ever-present brilliance of literature that emerges through the AKO Caine Prize entries, and ultimately the longlist and shortlist of the Prize, is both reassuring and inspiring. This year's shortlist, the 21st, was selected from over 200 entries from 28 countries and the African diaspora.

This year's judging panel had the distinction of being the first group of judges to convene and deliberate on the shortlist and winning story entirely online, with pleasing results. The judges who gave generously of their time, knowledge and discernment this year were Kenneth Tharp OBE, Executive Director of London's Africa Centre, journalist and broadcaster Audrey Brown, literary blogger James Murua, arts consultant and editor Ebisse Waka-jira-Rouw and the award-winning writer Gabriel Gbadamosi. The judging panel was energized by the enormous breadth and diversity of the entries for the Prize and by how much they challenged the notion of the African and diaspora experience, and its portrayal in fiction, as being one homogeneous whole.

The five shortlisted stories that you can read in this book are beautifully crafted and surprising creations, breathtaking in their variety, from satire and biting humour, to fiction based on non-fiction with themes spanning political shenanigans, outcast communities, superstition, loss and enduring love. They do much to illuminate the myriad ways there are to be African in the 21st century; and, while literature is neither biography nor always determined by biography, we are proud of the diverse backgrounds of the writers shortlisted for this year's prize, with a welcome first in the short-listing of a Rwandan/Namibian writer.

In the light of the Coronavirus pandemic, which interrupted plans for the customary literary week and award dinner where we announce the winner of the Prize, we have responded innovatively as an organization by initiating a series of podcasts, online literary events and partnerships, as well as by commissioning the British-Nigerian film-maker Joseph Adesunloye to produce our award announcement film. Our commitment has been very much to demonstrate that, even in extremely difficult times, African writers and African literature have much to say to illuminate our experience and make it bearable and understandable.

In this year, which has been particularly challenging for many of our beloved organizations in the artistic and cultural sector, we are immensely grateful for the support of our generous donors, supporters, partners, consultants, staff and trustees. Our particular thanks go to the principal sponsors of the 2020 Prize, the AKO Foundation, alongside the Oppenheimer Memorial Trust, the Sigrid Rausing Trust, John and Judy Niepold, Miles Morland Foundation, and Adam and Victoria Freudenheim. 'Other funders and partners include the British Council, Georgetown University (USA), the Lannan Center for Poetics and Social Practice, the van Agtmael Family Charitable Fund, Rupert and Clare McCammon, Arindam Bhattacherjee, Phillip Ihenacho and other generous donors.

We would like to express particular thanks to the AKO Foundation for their commitment to supporting the core costs of the Prize over the next three years, which we hope will enable us to respond robustly and creatively to both the challenges and opportunities of the present and the future.

Last but not least, we thank you, our readers and supporters, for your continued interest in supporting the best of literary talent from Africa and its Diaspora. We are grateful for this generous support without which the AKO Caine Prize would not be Africa's leading literary award.

Ellah P. Wakatama OBE, (Hon) FSRL
Chair of Trustees, the AKO Caine Prize
for African Writing

Dele Meiji Fatunla
Administrator, the AKO Caine Prize
for African Writing

Kenneth Olumuyiwa Tharp OBE
Chair of the Judging Panel, AKO Caine Prize
for African Writing 2020

The 2020 panel of judges

Kenneth Olumuyiwa Tharp OBE (chair) is a key figure in the UK arts and culture scene with over 35 years' professional experience in the sector. He began his career as a dancer; as one of the leading dance artists of his generation, he performed for 13 years with the internationally acclaimed London Contemporary Dance Theatre and then with other leading companies during a 25-year career as a performer, choreographer, teacher and director. From 2007 to 2016, he was Chief Executive of The Place, the UK's leading centre for contemporary dance development. He became Director of The Africa Centre in 2018.

Audrey Brown is a South African broadcast journalist, and one of the leading voices for the BBC World Service, presenting the flagship daily news and current affairs programme, Focus on Africa. She cut her journalistic teeth on progressive newspapers like *Vrye Weekblad* and the then *Weekly Mail* – now *Mail and Guardian* – in the late 1980s and early 1990s in South Africa. Audrey studied Film Criticism and Documentary Film Making at Varan Institute in Paris, and holds a BA Journalism degree from Rhodes University. She also studied for a Masters degree at the University of Wales College, Cardiff.

Gabriel Gbadamosi is an Irish-Nigerian poet and playwright. His London novel *Vauxhall* (2013) won the Tibor Jones Pageturner Prize and Best International Novel at the Sharjah Book Fair. He was AHRC Creative Fellow in British, European and African performance at the Pinter Centre, Goldsmiths, a Judith E Wilson Fellow for creative writing at Cambridge University and Royal Literary Fund Fellow at City & Guilds of London Art School, where he is now a Trustee. His plays include *Abolition* (Bristol Old Vic), *Eshu's Faust* (Jesus College, Cambridge), *Hotel Orpheu* (Schaubühne, Berlin), *Shango* (DNA, Amsterdam) and *Stop and Search* (Arcola Theatre).

James Murua is a Kenya-based blogger, journalist, podcaster and editor who has written for a variety of media outlets in a career spanning print, web and TV. He was editor for *The Star* newspaper in Kenya for five years and a columnist for nine where he was voted 'Columnist of the Year' in 2009. His online space jamesmurua.com, which focuses on literary news and reviews, was created in 2013 and is the number-one blog on African literature today. He won Best Writer on theatre, art and culture at Kenya's Sanaa Theatre Awards. His 'The African Literary Podcast' was nominated for Podcast of the Year at the Bloggers Association of Kenya Awards 2019.

Ebissé Wakjira-Rouw is an Ethiopian-born non-fiction editor, podcaster, publisher and policy advisor at the Dutch Council for Culture in the Netherlands. She co-founded Dipsaus, a podcast, online magazine, talent development platform and a publishing imprint with Uitgeverij Pluim. She has worked as a non-fiction editor at Uitgeverij AUP and co-edited the ground-breaking anthology, 'BLACK: Afro-European Literature in the Low Countries' (Dutch, 2017), the first of its kind available in the Dutch language. She is also a member of the curatorial team of the International Winternachten Literary Festival in The Hague.

The Caine Prize 2020
Shortlisted Stories

How to Marry an African President

Erica Sugo Anyadike

When you are interviewed for BBC documentaries in your palace, they will want to know how you met. Cast your eyes downward and tell them how you were a shy and hardworking secretary in the State House typing pool. Omit to mention that you were married. Lie that you were divorced and not looking. Not even for a President.

The truth is, when you meet, he will be neatly dressed. Shirt collar starched just so, shoes like shiny copper coins, fingernails trimmed and clean, hair clipped and precise as his speech. He will start by hanging around you a little too long. Your conversations will peter out and he will end them reluctantly. The other secretaries will stare. You'll pretend not to notice. Play it cool and coy. He will ask you out. Appear taken aback, smooth your skirt and shift your weight onto your other foot. He will look paternal and concerned. Explain that you are married, and he is too.

He will laugh and say he's only looking for a friend.

He will be lying.

Pay attention to his shoes. They will tell you everything.

Notice that when he comes by, he wears burgundy lace-ups. It will confuse you at first. A man like him is old-fashioned and into orthodox blacks and browns. Burgundy is his way of saying: an older man like me can still bring excitement to a young girl like you. Be sure to comment on his shoes. Remember – we all crave approval.

Listen to him talk about his wife. Part of you will like that he is respectful; *regretful,* even, that she will die from her illness and that there is nothing he can do about it. It is only a matter of time. Sympathize. But don't miss the opportunity. Mention how you wish you had a devoted loving husband such as him. He will probe, try to get you to say more. Grow sad and quiet. Later – drop hints about how you and your husband don't make love any more. Say: even women have needs. Giggle nervously, cover your mouth with your hand and apologize for being inappropriate. See his eyes brighten.

When he takes you out in the Mercedes, sink into butter-soft seats upholstered in cream. He will offer you a drink that appears almost magically from a console overlaid with the grain of an exotic wood, a burnished red-brown with dark streaks so opulent it's almost oppressive. Decline because good girls don't drink. Only later do they pretend to have acquired a reluctant palate for wine, courtesy of their husband's influence. He will signify his approval by putting his arm around your shoulders. See the watch on his wrist out of the corner of your eye: gold bezel, crocodile leather strap. Struggle to breathe. Do not panic. Money sometimes makes the air feel heavier for those who do not have it.

Stop attending night school and give up the English literature degree you were working towards. Being a consort requires being available at all hours. Like all powerful men, presidents have options, you must maximize your time.

Hear rumours swirling of how he was tortured in the Liberation struggle and how this may affect the consummation. These rumours are never said directly. Instead, those who have already identified you as a future benefactor will talk in circles. Cryptic conversations that are long and winding, yet deliberate like footpaths. Eventually, your aunt will tell you about modern medicine you can crush and slip into a man's tea; herbs for 'strength' that you can mix into a man's stew.

The first time you and the President make love, he will take you to an old colonial hotel with paint peeling like tears, as if mourning for its former glory. The doorman with the top hat will salute him, waiters will scurry and rush to bring him what he desires. When he orders high tea, think: he is more English than the English owner himself. Fail to understand the appeal of cucumber sandwiches. Murmur appreciatively as if you do. He will compliment the clotted cream that goes with the scones. The English hotelier, ruddy from the heat and frequent gin and tonics, will beam proudly. It is from one of his dairy farms, he'll say. His skin will be pink and thin, translucent like a lizard. His lips will be chapped, spittle congregating in the corners. He will undress you with his eyes. Later you'll hear a snatch of conversation and the hotelier will glance at you approvingly before leaning forward to whisper something in the President's ear. You won't hear much, just something like: *'You don't have to lie back and think of England with this one.'* The two men will laugh and the President will pat him on the back. This will only cement your dislike for the hotelier. He will go on a mental list you'll make. A list of what you hope to get, a list of people you will get back at.

It is only a matter of time.

When he finally takes you to bed, be prepared. The hotel room will have a four-poster bed and smell musty. Older women have gone before you, have navigated men like intrepid explorers braving unfamiliar terrain, have mapped out the ego of a man. They will warn you to strike a fine balance between Mary and Magdalene. They will guide you on how to signal desire while maintaining a certain reluctance that men of a certain age associate with modesty. To be too keen is unseemly. To appear uninterested can offend. Groom yourself, wear a delicate perfume and remember how much it seems to arouse him when you behave as if you are overwhelmed. Remember, he is a teacher. He'll want to teach you things. Act as eager to learn as you are to please.

Be ready to deal with the inevitable. He is four decades older than you, forty when you were born. Think: all presidents are men, no matter how god-like they seem. As such, they must suffer from the indignities of men. Conceal your surprise that your youthful flesh is enough. Hide the rush of power this gives you.

Afterwards – discuss what you are going to do about your husband.

Approximately six months later, your husband will be transferred. Or maybe he'll meet with a car accident. There has been talk in the newspapers of a mysterious black dog that appears in front of the cars of ministers who challenge the President. Engines explode, brakes fail. Political rivals make oblique references: be careful, make sure you don't see the black dog. Everyone knows what it means. You don't much care for your spouse but he is the father of your child. Feel relieved when the President tells you he's given your husband a posting far away. Years later, realize that you never saw or heard from your first husband again.

Fall pregnant. Weep. He will be ecstatic and reassure you he is looking forward to being a father. You'll have more children by him. He won't discriminate between the children you bear him and the one you already have. You'll ask for signs of your permanence in his life. He will dispense favours like tokens at an arcade. You'll be upgraded to a mansion, your relatives secured jobs without interviews, your every need met. You will be assigned a motorcade, given bodyguards. This will become a pesky problem later but in the beginning you will mock complain to your friends: imagine someone standing outside the bathroom when I need to use it! Recount with pretend dismay how everyone needed to be chased out of the bathroom first. This will be one of the last times you remember to show a semblance of shame.

His wife will die and he will insist on some decorum. A respectable period between her passing and his remarrying. By then you are already First Lady in everything but name and to salvage your wounded pride at having his children out of wedlock, he will promise you the wedding you want. Plan it scrupulously. You'll read bridal magazines, peruse dresses by

The wives of rich, well-travelled men will want to be your friends. If anybody sneers at you for being a secretary, then it will be done in whispers, behind walls. But out in the open, you will be feted. In restaurants, you'll be ushered into VIP sections. If you want anything, someone will be immediately dispatched to go and get it. And all you'll have to do is immerse yourself in charity work, open a few orphanages, kiss a few babies and accompany the President to state events.

This would be bearable if it wasn't so boring. Resent having all this money and looking like everybody else. Seem quiet and withdrawn when rubbing his feet. Remember your aunt's lesson: better to be wily than to whine. Tell him the wife of such a Big Man like him should be better dressed. Aren't you a reflection of him and his largesse? He will agree and a series of shopping trips will begin. You will travel overseas for haute couture, local fashion will not do for you. Have a personal shopper at Harrods. Jealous journalists will give you a nickname, something alliterative. You'll be proud of the moniker. It's catchy and has a ring to it. Draw the line at photographers. Have them assaulted for taking pictures carelessly. Words will be one thing but even you suspect that pictures are a bad idea. A drought does not mean you need to give up your Dior but perhaps it's best not to give your enemies too much ammunition. And you do have enemies, you do.

They are powerless – for the most part – but they are there.

Meet someone. He will shower you with attention and affection. Fall harder than you thought possible. Become focused on him and only him. Exchange endearments. Fantasize about a future together. Come up with codenames so you don't get caught. You call him John.

Someone will tell your husband. He will ask you outright if you're having an affair.

Deny this, fear stuck like a lump of mealie-meal in your throat.

Know: no-one betrays the President and gets away with it.

Warn your beloved.

John will travel, planning to stay out of the way until things cool down. You'll talk on public telephones, paranoid that someone has tapped the landlines. He'll become restless and want to return. Capitulate and admit that everything seems to have returned to normal. Though you feel the opposite, say: it is probably safe.

Arrange to meet. You'll wait at the appointed place for hours and hours, expectation souring your mouth like bad milk. He will not pitch. The next day you'll hear of his death. The President will deliver the news over breakfast, fake sympathy for John's family's loss while eating fried eggs. Hear the words 'car accident'. Bite your tongue to keep from crying. Under the table, you'll grasp the knife so hard that your palm will bleed. Stop eating for three days.

Conspiracy theories will swirl like fog and you'll wander around listlessly, asking questions to uncover answers you already know. You sense the whispers as you enter rooms, the words 'love affair', lingering in the air, the disapproval left behind like a bad stench. You'll walk around unable to mourn. The only permissible sign of your black mood will be the slow shuffling of your feet.

At your lover's funeral, neither his wife nor his brother will look at you although they're required to shake the President's hand. Adjust your dark sunglasses. Try to stem the tears without dabbing at your face too frequently. Angle your hat, taking care to tilt the round brim towards your chin to take the sharp edge off your emotions. The bad dreams will follow after his body enters the ground. Brace yourself. You'll feel scattered, emotions all over the place like flying ants after the rain.

You will see his face everywhere.

You will think you are being followed.

You will be right.

After a week you take to bed with a mysterious illness and he permits you to, even entering the bedroom to hold your cool hand and enquire solicitously about your health. The look in his eyes challenges you to cry openly or confess. You do neither.

Plot: your escape, your revenge, your next move.

Be an exemplary wife for months. Make cryptic comments about bad influences. Claim to have been misled. Convince him you have changed. He will forgive you. He will not know that you will never forgive him. By the time you'll ask him to secure your position as head of the Women's League, you'll have buttered him up sufficiently, having ensured that everything will be as he wants it, that his needs are met even before he realizes what he requires.

It's not solely the women's backing that you'll need. Acquire the support of youth leaders, mostly men. They are not dinosaurs like the sycophants that surround your husband; they are modern like you. None of them is over forty-five. Lavish them with gifts and business opportunities, let them glimpse what life would be like under your patronage. Ensure your popularity is entrenched. Speak at political rallies. Hear the applause grow louder at every one. Your ambition grows with it.

You'll do this over a matter of years. Slowly entrench your presence in the country's politics. See comprehension dawn on your enemies' faces as they realize how serious you are. Your husband is no longer the authoritarian figure he was, tall, forbidding, back ramrod straight. His shoulders droop, he falls asleep at the dinner table. Still, he is respected and revered. What he says counts and he has crowned you his political heir.

Watch army tanks roll in an inexorable march towards the presidential residence. Hear the onerous clank, the metallic tread on tarmac and realize that this is the soundtrack to your demise. Smell the teargas in the air, the scent burning your nostrils, pinpricks of moisture scalding your eyes. It will be a hot day but you will shiver, your blood congealing in your veins. Your husband will assure you, it is all for show: he is the head of the armed forces; they listen to him. Doubt him for the first time. You know how the army veterans hate you, you've heard the talk. Him they can forgive, they know his history, his credentials, but you'll be reduced to that thing between your legs, your only power that of a young woman to turn an old man's head. Chafe at this, it has always irked you, but that is of no consequence now. Attempt to rally your supporters. Arm a few members of the security force still loyal to the President. Consider that people may do many things for money but they are far more circumspect about being required to lose their lives. There will be no battle. Instead, a half-hearted resistance as you hole yourselves up inside State House.

They will take over the national broadcaster,

their hateful faces beaming into homes. They will claim it is not a coup. In truth, your husband will be ousted by the army generals who once enjoyed his favour. They will convene a meeting with him, treating him with deference, maintaining the illusion that they are 'negotiating' but it won't change the fact that there will be gunshots around your home, that you and your children will be crouched down in the kitchen, huddled and humiliated. One officer, bolder than the rest, will tell your husband that while they are sorry for betraying him, they could not allow you to ascend to his position. Even during the meeting, they will look around and you'll imagine them as vultures assessing your collection of expensive furniture as if it were carrion, calculating what they will take. Envisage corrupt Swiss bankers wondering when they can siphon the cash you have stashed away. You've heard the stories. You know what happened in the Congo.

It is only a matter of time.

You'll be spirited away in the dead of night, concerns for your safety finally upending your pride. He will call you from time to time; enquire about the children; meet you continents away when he has to travel for medical treatment but they will not chase him from his country like a dog.

They will invoke witchcraft to explain your

influence over him. You lured him; you are a siren; you dashed his legacy on the rocks. There will be calls for retribution, people will want you to do penance. You will not be just an African President's wife, you will be Eve and Delilah. You will be every temptress that ever lived, every bringer of bad things. They will absolve him of responsibility, his sins washed away in history, receding from memory the way waves retreat from the shore. He can stay, they will say, but you must leave.

Erica Sugo Anyadike is a Tanzanian writer based in Kenya. She began her career in South Africa as a screenwriter and worked in various capacities in the television sector. As a broadcaster, she created briefs and commissioned television series that dealt with issues such as apartheid, sexuality and gender. She continued that trend, when she began to produce her own content, never shying away from events and issues that intrigued her but always ensuring she kept her focus on characters, emotions and story. Apart from short films and television series, Erica has also written several short stories. In 2019, Erica was shortlisted for the Commonwealth Short Story Prize and the Queen Mary Wasafiri Writing Prize. Erica's interests lie in depicting complex African female characters and mentoring young filmmakers and writers. She is writing a novel and living in Kenya with her family. 'How to Marry an African President' was first published by addastories.org in 2019. Twitter: @SugoErica

What To Do When Your Child Brings Home A Mami Wata

Chikodili Emelumadu

Please note: 'Mami Wata' (also known in various other regions as 'Mammy Water') is used in this context as an umbrella term for both genders of the popular water entity (i.e. Mami and Papi Watas) and does not represent those other mer-creatures without the appearance of absolute humanoid traits. For these other non-humanistic water entities including but not restricted to: permanent mermaids and mermen, crocodile fellows, shark-brides, turtle crones and anomalous jelly blobs of indeterminate orientation, please see our companion volume, 'So You Want to Kill a Mer-Creature?' which will guide you through the appropriate juju framework to avoid or deflect repercussions and will elucidate general and specific appeasement rituals. See also, 'Entities and Non-entities: The Definitive Legal Position on Aquatic Interspecies Marriages, Non-Marriage Couplings and Groupings'.

Thank you for purchasing this material.

This paper is not meant to advocate any position, but merely to help guide you on whatever path you choose with regard to your child's new Mami Wata paramour, companion or girlfriend. We are working from the default position that your child is male and their partner is female, based on the statistics: the sheer numbers of Mami Watas coming out of bodies of water in recent times is well above the numbers of their male counterparts (a ratio of 5:1, compared to our human equivalent of 2:1[1]), as are the letters from mothers and potential mothers-in-law, which led to this book being written in the first instance. This is not to discount same-sex human/Wata relationships. However, these data have proven more difficult to collect and collate, as this group is more secretive and therefore difficult to access. This is due to the stiff penalties for Lesbian, Gay, Bisexual and Transsexual consortiums,[2] the supplementary punishment to the human party[3] in such associations and the threat of Dry-Out Tanks®[4] for the Mami Wata party.

Before we proceed, you must first of all administer the 'Mami Wata Tests' also known as the 'Mermaid Spirit Test' in a number of churches, a

---

1 McCain, C., 'Mami Wata Migration Census', December 2012.
2 Fourteen years' imprisonment in 24 non-sharia states of Nigeria, death by stoning in the 12 states practising sharia law.
3 An extra minimum of between two to five years, up to 25 years.
4 Developed by Innoson Group of Companies, in collaboration with the Ministry of Defence, Nigeria.

frankly misleading term, since it is well known that Mami and Papi Watas are very much corporeal and neither possess the permanent Piscean/sea-life lower extremities that mark one out as a mer-person.

The Tests

The first step is to establish whether your child's companion is benign or malevolent. Benign Mami Wata[5] (BMW) should need no help crossing the threshold to your abode, but evil cannot pass on its own and will often need help from an innocent or the owners of the house. An invitation to enter will not automatically bestow permission. Look out for common tricks such as broken heels (requiring someone to carry them over), tripping, stumbling or falling.[6]

As an aside, we recommend that parents ask to meet their children's paramour (or to use local parlance, 'kparakpo') or beau, as soon as things move past the dating stage. Malevolent Mami Wata[7] (MMW) are fond of public spaces: hotels,

---

5 Fig 1. Photo features real-life Mami Wata model (benign), reprinted with permission from the private libraries of Ms S. Ofili. Note the pleasant disposition and evenly scalloped edges of nacre-teeth.

6 See 'Christabel' by Samuel Taylor Coleridge.

7 Fig 2. No Mami or Papi Wata was harmed in this photo-shoot. Expiration of the biological process had already occurred prior to photography. Image courtesy of Department of Marine Biology and Limnology, Nnamdi Azikiwe University, Awka.

restaurants, bars and churches, to name a few. The upside is that, since Mami Watas are known to grant wealth to those on whom they bestow favour, one can be certain that one's offspring would not be squandering their financial resources on abortive ventures. But more on this later.

There are two main ways of checking the Mami Wata status of your child's current relationship:

a) **Mirror-Mirror**. Mami Watas are very beautiful and cannot resist the evidence of their own attractiveness. As such, they will stare at any reflective surface: windows, tumblers, pools of water collecting in the compound, and sometimes even spectacles. If your son's new girlfriend is looking you right in the eyes, chances are, she is not looking at you but at herself. This is your first sign.

b) **Fish and seafood**. This test is considered by many to be definitive, as we now know a Mami Wata will show aversion towards eating any of its kin from the sea. For indigenes of Rivers State, this testing has proven easiest to accomplish. Part of our research took us among the Ogba peoples of the aforementioned state, whose custom includes a practice of presenting shredded fish with kolanut for visitors, in place of the 'ose oji' peanut sauce of their Igbo neighbours. This means that any uncertainty is quickly laid to rest before the Mami or Papi Wata makes themselves at home – if it is not one's intention to welcome them.

Some of these beings have learnt to disguise their disinclination for fish and seafood under 'animal rights', 'vegetarianism' or otherwise 'veganism', but it is no matter. The fish or seafood need not be in whole flesh or lump form in order to be effective. As most Nigerian dishes entail the use of dried and ground crayfish, the test should be relatively easy to carry out. In its powdered state, crayfish or even ground shrimp will be undetectable to a human in trace amounts, and thus can be included in ose oji during kolanut-breaking rites. However, a Mami or Papi Wata would be able sense its presence, and it may reject the kolanut – a taboo and an insult to the host, which has its own ramifications. If the Mami Wata does go ahead to ingest the kolanut, there are signs to look out for.

Positive reactions to this test include:
I.   Itching: mouth, eyes, throat.
II.   Rashes or hives breaking out on the skin.
III. Vomiting.
IV.   Stomach cramps.
V.   Wheezing.
VI.   Swelling of any body parts: eyes, ears, stomach or throat.
VII. Optional: rolling of eyes and/or a sharp screaming – high-pitched enough to shatter glass objects.

These symptoms, argue the Independent Society

for the Integration of Sea Organisms (ISISO), are undiscernible from anaphylaxis, a severe human reaction to food or other substances to which one is allergic. They have pointed out the inhumanity of attempting an induction of said reaction. Nevertheless, one may obtain the appropriate medication from one's GP (or vet, if the GP does not, or will not administer antihistamines for use on Mami Wata). The difference between a MW-positive test and anaphylaxis is that administering an epi or Jext pen, Piriton or similar antihistamine, does not immediately halt the reaction in its tracks as it would in the case of anaphylaxis and will require further introduction of water-soluble Nutri X packs which mimic the salinity levels of the ocean.[8]

---

8 There are currently no known species of freshwater Mami Wata. Creatures which exist in these bodies of water are largely non-humanoid in nature. However, please be advised that entities known as 'sea gods' might dwell in various freshwater habitats. These are not to be confused with Mami and Papi Watas, for even though they bear a close resemblance to the former due to the amphibious nature of their existence, they can live for even longer periods on land and are not affected by seafood (even if they may have no fondness for it). Despite fantastical speculations by writers, e.g. Elechi Amadi in 'The Concubine' (Heinemann African Writers Series, 1989), investigations have shown that these 'sea gods' rarely have interest in human platonic and sexual relationships (preferring human veneration instead. See 'Efuru' by Flora Nwapa, Heinemann African Writers Series, 1966.) They also possess fully human hair, skin and teeth.

Again, you will need to ask your vet for the proper medication if your GP will not administer Nutri X for use on Mami Watas.

In the case of a malevolent Mami (MMW) or Papi Wata (MPW), people have been known to simply let them expire. This is a clear breach of ethics. Please administer the prerequisite treatment and dial your local Interspecies Department (ID) for further advice on removing the Mami Wata from your home, should you so desire.

Be advised that this does not always work and further action might be required. Your ID councillor will be able to provide you with help on this.

If you do not wish them to remain and would like to attempt a forceful ejection of an MMW or MPW from your home, see the section titled 'Forceful Ejection of a Mami or Papi Wata from Your Home,' in this booklet.[9]

Further testing

- Skimpy or revealing clothing: a Mami Wata is a slave to its own appearance and will often try to entice other men or women, even while

---

9 Be advised that a hypothesis has been posited and is currently undergoing some research as to Mami Watas and a manipulation of elements, and phenomena connected to water, even when such events may not occur in or around any body of water. These include but are not limited to: rain, rainstorms and hurricanes. See **Sharknado** film research by Levin, Thunder, NY, for further study and possible effects of this psycho-kinetic phenomenon.

they are with your son or daughter. Articles of clothing such as see-through blouses, tight trousers showing bulges (men), buttocks and thighs (women) and buttock-slits (both), singlets and vests in place of shirts, net vests, short shorts also known as 'batty riders' or 'pum-pum pushers', muscle shirts and deep V-necks (unisex) and dresses with cut-outs or overlong slits, are all possible signifiers.

- Check teeth for nacre. This is the crystalline substance which lends the insides of some shells their lustrous appearance. Teeth made from or coated with this substance tend to have more than one colour, resembling white or cream at first but often revealing, under sunlight, other colours on the spectrum: shimmering white, light pink or even a pale blue or green.

- Skin: the human skin is made up of diamond-shaped segments which can be seen without the aid of a microscope and can stretch out of this rhombus form as and when needed. The Wata creature's skin in comparison will have a smooth, almost plastic appearance. It will feel like skin (some studies describe the texture as silicon) but further investigation will reveal no pores or hairs. Under a microscope, a stacked plate-like or disc-like appearance to the skin, similar to scales, will be present.

- Water consumption: due to this lack of breatha-bility to the skin (it has been hypothesized that this is to prevent the Mami Wata losing much of its own bodily fluids/cell material through osmosis while in saltwater) the Wata organism will consume large quantities of water as – even though it is possible for it to spend long periods on land – it tends to overheat. It is in this regulation of its body temperature that it most resembles its distant cousin, the fish, since its temperature tends to rise and fall according to its surroundings. Furthermore, a Mami Wata will look simply breathtaking when submerged or drenched with water, in a way that is humanly impossible (a noticeable lack of puckering to extremities, absence of goose pimples, and a lack of the greying or matting qualities which plagues Homo Sapiens upon long hours of submersion. Hair simply falls back into place and is not subject to 'shrinkage' as is the case with natural afro hair.) Please note that this booklet does not advocate the illegal practice of 'Splashing'[10] (an exercise advocated by The Children of Men [TCoM], a quasi-religious group) in order to force a Mami or Papi Wata to reveal its true nature. This is an erroneous exercise (due to the fact that Mami Wata, as mentioned, will not have fishy extremities) which has led to inappropriate necklacing in the recent past.

- Lights, Camera, Action: a Mami Wata captured

---

10 See film *Splash*, Howard, Ron, 1984.

on film is unlike any human image ever seen, natural or enhanced. As they are always flawless and HD-ready, their image when captured on film or digital is even more so. The resultant photograph should emit a blurriness/ glow around the edges, much like the phosphorescence of some sea creatures. Or there might be a yellow or pink eye (a relation to the human 'red eye' syndrome). Do not adjust your settings after the first one or two photos as the fault does not lie in your camera, but in the entity posing before it (and Mami Wata enjoy and execute poses in varying degrees of artistic perfection, naturally making use of space and light in the creative manner of trained photographers). Resultant snapshots are often well balanced in perspective and composition.

- Inappropriate jewellery: earrings on men, belly rings, studs in arms, lower back, too many rings on ears, toe rings and ankle chains, etc. Any jewellery which a normal Nigerian would not wear. Also watch out for an over-groomed appearance on men: too-neat eyebrows, precision haircuts, also known as 'Fades', sheeny skin and blueprint or landscaped facial hair.

To welcome or not to welcome?

Upon conclusion of the tests (as many as one deems necessary to prove or disprove the presence of a Mami/Papi Wata in their home), we come to the next step.

Welcoming

Should you choose to welcome a Mami Wata, officially, into your home, there are certain items which will achieve the desired effect.

- Eggs: Mami Watas love to eat eggs. Chicken eggs will do in a pinch, but more unusual eggs are sure to bestow the Mami Wata's favour upon you. Quails' eggs, ducks' eggs and guinea-fowl eggs can be obtained from most parts of Nigeria comfortably. Some wealthier families have been known to purchase ostrich, eagle and falcon eggs for their consumption. Vulture and owl eggs are acceptable too due to their rarity, although you may need to contact The Association of Witches' Familiars of Nigeria (AWFN) for the latter, if you are to avoid a clash with the covens of your area. Human eggs are NOT ACCEPTABLE so please do not try this, even though there exists a black market for the self-same purpose. Ingesting human products is prohibited under the 'Cannibalism and Consumption of Human Products Act, 2003' of the Nigerian constitution and is NOT covered under the 1999 constitution of 'Right to Religion' as many black/red marketers would have you believe.

  Humans caught supplying Mami Wata with organs for consumption will be penalized under section 423a of the aforementioned Act. The penalty is death.

- Mirrors and trinkets. As mentioned, Mami and

Papi Watas enjoy gazing upon their reflections. Presentation of a mirror of any size indicates a welcome, as do trinkets and baubles, jewellery, make-up and clothing. These items need not be too costly, but should be presented properly in order to reveal willingness.

- Exotic fruits. Apples, lychees, kiwis, pomegranate, passionfruit, persimmon and various berries signify an acceptance. Of course, one may choose to go in the other direction and source fruits which used to be local to the area but may have died out due to a cultivation of fast-yielding crops and imported varieties. Think ugili (*Irvingia Gabonesis*), udala (white star apple, also known as 'agbalumo'), velvet tamarind and the Nigerian pink apple.

- Oils and incenses. Again, varieties not often seen in Nigeria are welcome, although any would do in a pinch as long as they are beautifully presented. An informal vox among our volunteers reveals palm kernel oil to be a favourite, closely followed by breadfruit seed oil.

- Cloth: lace, ankara, damask, Jacquard. Please note, the more expensive the gift, the stronger the likelihood of crossing over into Bridal Gift territory –unless this is one's intention. While Mami Wata are often keen on human relationships over their Wata counterpart, it does not help for one to overwhelm them, as a benign Mami or Papi would often flee if it sensed a trap, i.e. people who seek to use it for purely financial gain. Bear in mind that a marriage conducted for naturalization would only confer this privilege on any resultant offspring. Citizenship for the Wata creature would be by registration and involves renouncing any other citizenships to other kingdoms or realms.[11] Citizenship by registration is only valid in male-female, human/Wata relationships, where the human partner is male. Please contact your local Interspecies Department (ID) for pointers and clarification.

- Cameras, smartphones and selfie sticks. There has been an increase in demand for the last in recent times, leading to a boom in home-grown manufacturing of the item, as well as an increase in Chinese importation of same. Giving them means to capture, replay or review their images is viewed as a positive step.

Rejection

The following are ways of showing displeasure at your child's Mami Wata companion and thus, your rejection of them.

- Sand. Pouring sand in any food you offer them is a way of showing your preference for a terra-based relationship for your offspring. Popular dishes include but are not limited to: garri or eba, any fufu, soup and jollof rice. Some families are fond of including small

---

11 'Multiple Citizenship in Nigeria'.

stones in such messages, but not only is this unnecessary, it is detrimental as well. Simple sand should suffice as a deterrent, without the need to injure the creatures' nacre dentition.

- Ululation. Often preceded by three claps, ululation has the added advantage of summoning neighbours and witnesses, especially in the case of a malevolent Mami Wata rejection. This is especially useful if a need arises for police statements and the like.
- Shouting, weeping and striking of the breast: one's own breast, not the Mami Wata's, which may bring about the opposite effect. This step is self-explanatory.

Forceful ejection of a malevolent Mami or Papi Wata from your home

Even the most benign Mami Wata is proud, so a rejection of a MW, either benign or malevolent, will most likely be met with compliance, however grudging.

Still, there are some cases where force will have to be applied. These are when a Mami Wata has:

a) Already tied life essences with your offspring;

b) If said offspring has voluntarily surrendered their reproductive facilities or libido, known colloquially as 'Conji';[12] or

---

12 Please see a free sample of our eBook 'Untying a Surrendered ConjiKnot' click <u>here</u>.

c) If the Mami or Papi Wata, by nature of its malevolence, simply refuses to leave. The first step is to report to your local ID branch, but if this fails to resolve the issue then:

• Fire. As an elemental opposite of water, fire is an antithesis to the Mami Wata. A word of caution: this is best done where the MW has no access to water in order to put out the fire and/or blast/crush perceived tormentors with high-pressure streams and walls of water. They may also call other dangerous amphibious mer-creatures[13] to lend assistance and destructive capabilities.

• Blood. This calls for the slaughter of other sea-born creatures in the vicinity from which the Mami or Papi Wata is refusing to budge. This killing is preferably performed outside the abode and the blood of the slaughtered sea creature smeared as a deterrent on the walls, streetlamps and roads leading up to (or away from) the abode. As a Wata being will most likely mourn the death of one of its cousins, this should lead it away from its current location. Please note that, in instances where Conji has been surrendered or sea marriage taken place, this will most likely mean driving one's offspring away with the Mami Wata. It

---

13 See 'Attack and Defence: How to Prevent Retaliation by Malevolent Water Beings' by Mazi O.O. Emenanjo, Kachifo, 2014.'

may be wise to attempt an untying first.
- Forceful ejections by the Interspecies Department. This is performed by the correctional arm of the ID and is self-explanatory.

In conclusion

This information sheet is intended as a basic guide to help you navigate the often choppy waters of the recent trend of interspecies relationships. But ultimately, that is what it is, a guide. It is not intended to be taken as law, since Mami Wata relationships differ on a case-by-case basis. Only you can decide what to do, based on your own unique experience. As a point of note, 5,000 respondents were polled when Mami Watas started to make themselves known in 2011. Out of these, 97% unequivocally condemned interspecies relationships, while 3% were undecided. That figure is now down to 72% with 5% still in the undecided camp, and 23% in the 'Yes' category.

This appears to indicate that feelings about Mami Watas are still in flux and likely to change further. Whatever action you take, it may be best to leave yourself some wiggle room, in case a new experience with the Wata breed leads to a change in your opinion.

Chikodili Emelumadu was born in Worksop, Nottinghamshire and raised in Nigeria. Her work has previously been shortlisted for the Shirley Jackson Awards (2015), the Caine Prize for African Literature

(2017) and a Nommo award (2020). In 2019, she won the inaugural Curtis Brown First Novel prize for her novel 'Dazzling'. 'What To Do When Your Child Brings Home A Mami Wata' was first published in *The Shadow Booth*, volume 2 (2018).
Twitter: @chemelumadu

that Benji, her husband, had finally returned. The lock clicked. Benji still had his keys. He didn't turn on the light when he entered. Belt buckle clanking, zipper running, and the rustle of clothes falling to the ground: when you are sixty-seven years of age and have shared nearly fifty of those with the same person, you can tell his intentions by the sounds he makes. The carved cupboard of Sapele mahogany and the wall beside it caught Benji's shadow shifting in the lantern's low-trimmed light. It seemed to her that he stood in the gap of the screen curtain, his eyelids heavy with fatigue, as if he'd paddled through miles of smoky streams to get here. She'd always known he'd return, she'd waited for him to come home, as he always did – straight from the workshop, pausing before joining her to check on little Alice; or, perhaps, after a brief stop at Uduak's drinking table where, with his friends, he would knock back shots of schnapps imbued with medicinal roots, bark of trees known to restore vitality and provoke desire in men young and old. With his clothes hooked on the back of a chair in the hallway, he would walk into the bedroom naked as day, the old scar on his arm gleaming.

She shifted on the bed and made room, and Benji met her – loose, sprawled, arched, with parted lips – and then pressed his body against hers. She caught the whiff of dry wood, sweat and handsaw grease. His calloused hands slid round her neck, then cupped her face. His lips shook as his eyes hovered over hers. She took his lower lip into her mouth, calmed it. He was caressing her face with one hand, and with the other he undid the wrapper tied around her waist and flung it into the dark where a clatter followed the tumbling items on the nightstand, then lowered his head over her belly and navel, making his way down the soft trail of hair.

He stayed there until she retrieved herself with a sharp moan, turning sideways, like a bitch shrugging off her young. She turned and, pressing his shoulders until he was on his back, descended on him. With his balls secure in her mouth, she held Benji until she heard him plead, his voice drifting out the window. She relented, and then raised herself until they were facing each other, breathing the same air. He turned sharply as she slid beneath him. With her arm hooked over his neck, she drew her knees up, and held her thighs open like a funnel. In countless heated strokes that ran along the channels of her body, he came in a roar. Afterward, in the deep dark, they lay silent.

He was gone by the morning. When she rose, the pale green walls of the room seemed unfamiliar. She glanced at the old sewing machine, piled with plain cotton and linen, rolls of muslin and gingham, yards of blue-black adire. The handbags on the wardrobe were still untouched in their nylon wrappings. It all came back to her. Alice bringing gifts every time she visited, gifts Nimi hardly touched. Hollow days. She had moved from the bedroom and slept instead on the narrow bed in the sewing room. Last week, when Alice visited with her husband Asari and their two boys, Nimi prodded them to leave some clothing behind so they could travel light on their subsequent visits. Alice and Asari had asked again if they could find her a new place, somewhere closer to where they lived at Wimpey, but Nimi had said no, she did not want to move.

Now she sat up in bed with her back resting on the wall. Her neighbour Ibifuro was singing in the courtyard, a melodious and militant church chorus. Ibifuro lived in the flat across, with her three children and husband Enefa – a safety technician on an oil platform in Bonny. Nimi parted the curtain and peered at the tall woman. She was bent over a basin, hands vigorously washing clothes, and her swirling voice trembled: *I will sing unto the Lord, for he has triumphed gloriously, the horse and rider thrown into the sea.*

Nimi let the curtain drop. She got out of bed and slipped her feet into the plastic sandals she reserved for the outside. The door whistled on its hinges when she pulled it, and the day swung open before her. The yard was already swept. Normally she rose early to do this and some other chores before her neighbours got up.

You are sleeping well these days, Ibifuro called out.

You are washing, she replied warmly but in no mood for playful banter. How was your night?

We thank God, Ibifuro sighed.

Nimi waited as Ibifuro dunked the striped shirt in her hands back into the basin's foaming water and began to hum the same church chorus, gravely.

You know that woman Dauta, Ibifuro said, that one who calls herself a caterer. You know I introduced her to my friend whose son was getting married.

Nimi could not recall hearing about this Dauta, but from Ibifuro's tone she could tell the introduction had now produced undesirable outcomes.

So imagine how I felt, Ibifuro continued, when I woke up this morning to see messages from my friend and voice messages from people I don't know, that the caterer I brought spoilt their occasion, that food did not go round.

I hate when I'm at a wedding and that happens, Nimi said.

So I called Dauta to ask what happened, and you won't believe it, the woman told me it's not her fault that they paid her to cook for only one hundred people but expected the food to cover nearly three hundred guests present at the reception.

Is that the bad tongue she used to answer you? Nimi asked in disgust.

Ibifuro clucked, as if still shocked at the woman's rudeness. She was not the type of person to stand by and watch her integrity and good name get sullied.

No need to make trouble, Nimi cautioned.

Ibifuro waved it off with a carefree hand. She said, I am going to the pharmacy later, on my way I will stop by her house so I can hear all she has to say to me, and then I'll know what to do. I don't have time to make trouble.

Nimi imagined the wedding reception, held outdoors on a field with colourful canopies or a large tent, a highlife gospel band in full swing, guests in their best clothes, while the bride and groom sat smiling on their special seats, passing a flute of champagne to each other and unaware of the shortage of food and the quiet departures, the cars turning out of the parking lot, taxis flagged down in haste, the small groups walking toward the nearest bus stop. Very unpleasant, Nimi thought. Even at funerals, eating and drinking carried on through the day and into night.

Benji returned to me last night, she said.

Ibifuro's head was down facing the basin. She did not turn around or ask any worried questions. Instead she retrieved a submerged shirt, squeezed and dropped it into another basin filled with clean water.

Nimi, undecided, weighed if she should repeat what she'd just said.

Ibifuro had been there the day the news came about Benji. The two women were shelling egusi in the yard when Chima and Chidi, two men who ran their metalwork stores next to Benji's, arrived to say Benji had been hit by a motorbike crossing Ikwerre Road and was in the hospital. They were remarkably short and stout and good-natured, these men. Nimi and Benji often spoke about them, how they possessed good names in the wrought-iron business, how they plied their trade to complement each other's skills, did not quarrel over customers, how their grit and ambition never excluded warmth. Together the three of them sped along in a taxi towards Braithwaite Memorial Hospital. They did not explain to Nimi why they avoided the main entrance to the hospital and led her instead towards a bungalow at the back. The pathway was lined with hedges of ixora, blood red and radiant. Her nostrils flinched at the strong smell of formaldehyde. The two men stopped walking as they came in full view of the building, and Chidi placed a hand on her shoulder.

What is happening? Nimi asked.

She got no response.

The flower hedges slipped fast before her eyes, the ground was giving way beneath her, her hand slammed against Chidi's chest and grasped his shirt collar tight. His eyes were bloodshot. Madam, madam, he kept saying to her. Chima tried to restrain and console her, but she broke free from them and ran to see where Benji, wearing the shirt Nimi had made from adire cloth with circular patterns running in blue and dead-leaf green, lay lifeless on the stretcher.

As she watched Ibifuro peg her washing on the line, she could taste again Benji's sour morning breath on her tongue. She could still feel on her waist the firm grip of his hands, from where he'd lifted her while on his knees last night, gently, easily, and she reckoned with the words of her people that when we return we do so in the vigour of youth.

Benji came to see me last night, Nimi repeated.

Ibifuro swung round towards Nimi – the bulk of the woman, breasts swaying under her nightdress. A white plastic peg slid out of her hand, but she kept her eyes fixed on Nimi.

Mama, Ibifuro pleaded.

Nimi looked away. She knew what would follow. Ibifuro would immediately call or text Alice, and she would come over. Pastor Osagie would casually drop in the next day to *spend time* with Nimi. The church's women's group would pick an afternoon to lavish her, cleaning and sweeping, preparing meals for her that would go to waste, while dishing out admonitions. By the weekend, the youth group would gather, singing lustily in her sitting room and offering prayers for blessings on her behalf. All of these she would receive with gratitude, but they would be beside the point.

I saw him only in my dream, Nimi said with a light voice. It gave me comfort.

She took out a napkin and dusted the Formica

sideboards and the obeche cabinet in her front room, folded her wrappers and hung her gowns up in the wardrobe in an arrangement she liked. And then she swept the floor of the whole house. There was to be a meeting in church that evening so she sent word she would not make it, claiming an emergency had occurred. Nimi remembered that look she saw on Ibifuro's face when she told her of Benji's return. She thought of her own sleepy-eyed astonishment when she awoke that morning to a bed in disarray. A current ran down her spine. If it was a crack in her mind that had let Benji back into the world, she thought, then her intention was to keep the crack open, widen it. Her plan was to visit the evening market, and then make stew. She knew that if you love a person and they love you back, you can cook for them something that ensures they find their way to you, should they be lost.

It was a little before five when she stepped out of the house and into the street. The sky over Eliozu was alive with an orange light. The slanted, rusty roofs of the houses downhill glinted like gold. With her shopping bag in hand, she closed the gate quietly behind. Alagbo's sky-blue Nissan Sunny was shimmering at his gate and blocking the entrance, finally back from the mechanic after three solid months of delayed salary. Alagbo had complained about the dire state of things, the cost of a new engine block, and the craftiness of motor mechanics. Nimi made a mental note to call in later to salute him, to greet his family, and to thank God with them that things turned out fine. Chituru sat on a high stool in front of his DVD store, watching two other men play draughts, the pieces sliding and spilling noisily on the wooden board.

Out on the main road Nimi turned toward the market. It was that time just before nightfall when people were on their way home from work, when the air darkened and the figures milling in the markets and the streets may not be people at all. Her eye caught an ice-cream man pedalling home on his bicycle; he was done for the day, no bell ringing, no driving the children mad with want. She felt awake to her own footfalls, to the bright green and yellow headscarf on the woman walking ahead, to the rising murmur of the market as she approached, and to the cars tooting their horns, beetling along in the rush-hour traffic.

She weaved her way through the crowd, side-stepped puddles, steered clear of the man pushing a wheelbarrow loaded with sacks of onions and grunting, *Chance, chance.* The stalls at the very end of the market were the ones she wanted.

Crabs in woven baskets were clacking away and waving their claws, the giant snails gliding in open buckets, and rows and rows of tables were laid out with tilapia, brown snapper, frozen mackerel wrenched out of misty cartons, silversides and bonga, mudskippers fresh from the river, bulgy-eyed, thrashing on the table and gasping for breath. Nimi stopped to admire a heaped bowl of peppers – blemish-free, slender and green.

Take two bowls for the price of one, said the young woman in the shed. A nod went from seller to buyer.

Thank you my daughter, Nimi said. Even the night market was in alliance with her.

When Nimi and Benji were young, before Alice was born, they lived in a little house far outside of town on East-West Road. Benji's workshop was right at the front veranda. People were reluctant to commit to a young, newly arrived carpenter, and there was no denying it, to get those jobs, Benji often exaggerated his experience, inflated the number of years of practice under his belt: *I can do it, Ma. I have built that type of armchair before, sir.* And he delivered the jobs, not one complaint followed. Still, it was her petty trading that had kept them from starving or returning to the village until he started getting the sort of customers who drove in cars and dropped by the workshop with their children dressed in school uniforms. Then she sold the first set of throw pillows and tablecloths that she ever made. She made headrests and armrests, tablecloths with placemats to match. Nimi sat and sewed, recalling needlework techniques from primary school, adding a flourish to the patterns here and there, with the sound of Benji's hammering and sawing going in the background, until evening when they packed up and turned in to nest. They stayed up late in those days, talking about she couldn't remember what, long after they had relished the crumbly purity of boiled yam dipped in fire-warmed palm oil and sprinkled with salt. When they stayed up late enough to crave a snack before sleep, Benji would, in no time at all, put together fresh corn, roasted golden, which they ate with ube, buttery and delicate. On one of those nights, while they lay in bed – this was the moment Nimi held in her mind as she scanned rows of fresh tomatoes in the market – Benji pressed his knee into the hollow of her own, slid his foot's instep into the arch of her sole, and said: me and you.

Nimi rolled over and faced him.

When I come back, he said, in our next life, I will find you.

What surprised her was that he had said the words out loud: she had found him to be a man who promised little but did much more.

I will look for you too, she said. That way it will take us half the time.

Lights began to appear in the neighbours' houses as Nimi approached the gate. It had begun to drizzle, quickly hardening into storm. Once she stepped inside her house, she set her shopping bags down, and then she found a towel to wipe her face and arms.

Ignoring the words of the landlord, she made a

fire with real firewood, opening the windows to let out the smoke. It would have hastened things to have two pots going, but she was in no rush. She took down a tray and laid out the smoked catfish, the fresh prawns, the periwinkles, the water snails and the clams. She chopped a fat onion and dropped it into the hot oil. It spat like loud applause. She pulled a log from the fire to reduce the heat. She turned the contents of the tray into a large pot and set it aside. With the onions still sizzling, she poured in a bowl of fresh peppers and tomatoes already blended together for a fee at the market. She let it cook for a while. The aroma filled the room and tickled her nostrils. Last night while they caught their breaths, Benji had put his nose against her hair and inhaled. He had always been stirred by the scent of utazi. From the shelf, she lowered a plastic container where she stored condiments – dried mint, ukashi, uda, utazi, uziza – and crushed some dry utazi leaves into the stew. The fire crackled, and the pot boiled. She unknotted her headscarf and flung it aside. Tonight, after they had eaten the stew with slices of boiled yam, there would be time left to talk.

Early the next morning Ibifuro knocked on her door. Nimi cracked it open just enough to show she was available for a brief exchange and nothing more. Through the gap, Ibifuro stretched her hand and offered her a pack of vitamin tablets, a gift from her visit to the pharmacy. She reached out for the pills, the door slipped open wider, and Ibifuro's eyes strayed from Nimi's face to the room behind her.

Ibifuro stood back and said: I heard voices last night.

I was watching a film, Nimi replied. Her voice resolved, like a teenager who understood the question from a parent but was playing by her own rules.

Ah, okay, Ibifuro said. Only two people talked in the film?

Yes, Nimi replied.

And just then, one of Ibifuro's children called for her mother.

Let me hurry, she said. I will see you when I return.

Go well, Nimi said and closed the door.

Nimi emerged later to sweep the yard. She found a cutlass and did some weeding out back. She washed the drums Ibifuro's family used to collect rainwater. Then she went inside, unearthed her sewing kit from underneath a pile of fabric in the wardrobe, and began to stitch a fresh pattern. Late in the afternoon, in the vanishing light, she called Alice. One of the boys picked up and shrieked hello, and before Nimi could say hello back, he passed the phone to his mother, who sounded cheerful and distracted in the din. Nimi spoke to each of them unhurriedly. All her day they could have; the night was hers alone to keep.

Jowhor Ile was born and raised in Nigeria. He is known for his first novel, *And After Many Days*. In 2016, the novel was awarded the Etisalat Prize for Literature. His short fiction has appeared in *The Sewanee Review*, *McSweeney's Quarterly* and *Litro Magazine*. He earned his MFA at Boston University and is currently a visiting professor at West Virginia. He splits his time between Nigeria and the US. 'Fisherman's Stew' was first published in *The Sewanee Review* in 2019.

Twitter: @JowhorIle

The Neighbourhood Watch

Rémy Ngamije

Mondays: Auasblick, Olympia and Suiderhof (maybe Pionierspark)

Elias roughly shakes everyone awake. For breakfast, a chorus of yawns sprinkled with stretching. There is some grumbling. Then everyone starts folding their blankets and pieces of cardboard. A can of water is passed around. Everyone cups a handful and splashes their faces. Elias goes first, then Lazarus, then Silas, and then Omagano. There is little left when it reaches Martin, the newest and youngest member of the Neighbourhood Watch. When the can is empty it is stashed away with the other valuables in a nook under the concrete abutment of the bridge. The bridge's underside is precious real estate. When it rains it remains dry and in winter it wards off some of the cold. More than once it has been defended against a rival posse. It belongs to the Neighbourhood Watch now and everyone else tends to leave it alone. The 'NW' sprayed onto the bridge's supporting columns has the same effect as musty pee at the edge of a leopard's territory. It promises bloody reprisal if any encroachment is made onto the land. The Neighbourhood Watch's hidden stash is as safe as their fierce reputation and basic street common sense permits it to be. Generally, stealing is frowned upon. Stealing is bad because it makes everything a free-for-all and then everyone has to lug their scant possessions around to protect them. More luggage means slower foraging. It also means pushing one's poverty around in broad daylight. Nobody likes a thief.

The light of day is not full-born when they set out. Elias, the oldest and the leader, sets out with his lieutenant, Lazarus. Omagano goes with them, trying to straighten the kinks in her hair, using her fingers as comb teeth. They head to town since they have the best clothes and will not stand out too much or draw the ire of the city police patrols or the judging stares of security guards. If they walk slowly enough other pedestrians will not catch their stench. On any given day they have a multitude of things to worry about and shame is one of the first things a person learns to shed on the street. But smelling bad is something they try to avoid as much as possible. People's eyes can accept a man in tattered, browned and dirty clothing, even in a store or a church. But a smelly man is despised everywhere.

Elias knows most of the kitchen staff in the city's hotels and restaurants. They call him

Soldier or Captain. Sometimes the staff leave out produce about to turn for him and his group. Some potatoes with broken skins, mangoes which dimple at the slightest pressure, or wrinkled carrots. When they are feeling especially kind the cooks give him some smushed leftovers from the previous night in styrofoam containers – half-eaten burgers, chips drowning in sauce, salads picked clean of feta. But that is only sometimes. The kitchen staff have to squirrel away leftovers for their own families so often there is little left for them to put aside for Elias.

The real prizes are the overflowing bins behind the restaurants. In the early morning, with steam billowing around vents, with the bins laden with last night's throwaways, it is possible to get lucky and find some edible, semi-fresh morsels. By late morning, the sun turns them into rotting compost heaps. The Neighbourhood Watch knows: the early bird does not catch the worms. Elias, Lazarus and Omagano lengthen their strides to get to town in time.

Elias has a racking cough. He pulls the mucus through the back of his mouth and arcs a dollop away where it lands with a plop. The cough becomes worse each day. Sometimes there is blood in the gunk from his chest but he waves everyone's concerns away. Blood is a part of life. Blood is a part of death. He does not argue with his biology. His greying hair is unevenly cut but not so much that it draws attention. Omagano managed to do a decent job with the scissors.

Lazarus walks behind him, alert, leathery limbs toughened and blackened. At first glance his tattoos are invisible. But upon closer inspection the shoddy work of an unsteady needle and a rudimentary grasp of illustration are seen on his forearms and biceps. They look more like scars than artwork. His ferret face scans his surroundings, always on the lookout for a bin, or marks that let them know they are encroaching upon rival territory. In general, the CBD is an open supermarket for everyone. But sometimes young upstarts try to cordon off particularly fruitful blocks or alleys. Sometimes they become brazen and will beat up an old man they find rooting around in a bin. They would be foolish to try that with Lazarus. His presence in a fight drastically changes the bookies' odds.

Omagano brings up the rear, her frame thinned and stripped of fat, collarbones shining beneath her spaghetti-strap top, nipples sometimes showing their topography through the thin material, still as passably pretty as the day she joined them. Small children are the most valuable recruits. They are nimble and loyal and when you get them young enough the possibilities are endless. Women come next. Sometimes the rubbish bins the Neighbourhood Watch visits are fenced off. Guards threaten to beat them for trespassing. Sometimes they want a bribe. Ten dollars, twenty when they know the bins have a high yield (if they have not rifled through them themselves already). When Elias has the money, he pays it. When he does not and they really need to find food Omagano goes behind a dumpster with a guard and does what needs to be done. The three of them are always on food duty.

Silas and Martin look for other essentials. Discarded blankets and mattresses, rent clothing, useable shoes, broken crates, trolleys, toothpaste tubes worth the squeeze, slivers of soap, pipes and pieces of wire, and anything that can burn. They loiter around construction sites and in shopping-mall parking lots looking for something to filch. Wheelbarrows are useful, but nothing beats a trolley. When a trolley is unattended outside a store they push it out of sight quickly. If they find someone in need of a trolley they trade it for something useful. If not, they wheel it back to the bridge. So far they have three trolleys, but they are not too eager to add to their collection. Trolleys take up space and their value can embolden thieves.

Silas likes risk. He has a habit of discovering things that have had previous owners. Like cellphones.

'Where did you get that?' Elias will ask.

'Discovered it,' Silas will reply. Shrug of the shoulders, curl of the lip.

Elias constantly warns him not to be a Christopher Columbus and Lazarus threatens him, but there is nothing to be done about it. Silas steals. If he finds something worth selling then they share the proceeds. But if he gets caught stealing and is beaten or arrested then he had it coming. He is short and skinny but he screams danger to anyone who knows what to look for. A cocksure walk, an impish grin, eyes that never look away and hands that hover over a certain pocket when the talk around him gets too rough. Martin follows him around, learning the codes of the street, trying to look tough too, which is hard to do when he has to pull his baggy trousers up every couple of steps. The width of the streets, the height of the buildings and the number of people walking around still amaze him. Silas says he will get used to it all after a while.

The two groups work separately and meet up in the late afternoon. The food crew shares the lunch. Half a loaf of brown bread, some salty mashed potatoes, soft grapes and some water. The valuables crew has a stack of newspapers, plastic piping and two battered, floppy poorboy caps. Elias tries on one, Lazarus takes the other.

'Auasblick tonight,' Elias says when they finish eating. 'Get some sleep now.'

It is too hot to be on the streets now. Night is a better and more lucrative time for the Neighbourhood Watch.

Auasblick is nice. They still know how to throw away things there. If they hit the bins early enough they can score some good things. Broken toasters, blenders, kettles, water bottles, teflon pots or pans scrubbed raw and rendered common and cheap, giant flatscreen television cardboard boxes and, maybe, some food. Omagano and Martin will push the trolley. Elias, Lazarus and Silas will scout ahead, opening bins, perusing the wares, gauging the value of the detritus of suburbia.

The only problem with Auasblick is how far it is. The further the city spreads itself out the further the foragers have to go. And Auasblick is getting fat, it is already spilling over its sides. New plots are going up for sale, tractors gnaw into steep hillsides. The bountiful weekly dustbin harvest there means more and more crews are creeping in. Soon it will be overcrowded. Like Olympia and Suiderhof. Pionierspark used to be worthwhile, but these days it is not. Too many heads peeking through curtains to find the source of disturbances, too many dogs barking, too many patrolling vehicles with angry, shouting men.

— '*Blerrie kaffirs. Gaan weg!*' The earlier the Neighbourhood Watch can get to Auasblick the better. *Auasblick is die beeste vullisblik.*

Tuesdays and Thursdays, In Days Past: Katutura, Hakahana, Goreangab, Wanaheda and Okuryangava

Poor people only throw away garbage. And babies. Garbage is disgusting, babies are useless. That is why the Neighbourhood Watch have stopped scavenging on the other side of town.

When Elias and Lazarus were just starting out they used to flick through every bin they could find in every suburb they could reach, walking blisters onto their feet and holes into their shoes. They were indiscriminate and desperate and always hungry. Every bin was fair game. Elias had been by himself for a long time before he met Lazarus. Finding enough to eat and all of the other paraphernalia he needed to survive a day on the streets by himself was taxing. When he proposed an alliance, in the light of a burning drum under a bridge in town, Lazarus was hesitant at first. Lazarus was doing just fine by himself. To team up with an old man like Elias was not an ideal situation. But few things are as persuasive as the fangs of winter. It forced them to work together. Two people could cover more ground. Also, if they specialized – one for food, one for other essentials – they could do a lot more in a day. It made sense, and it worked for them. Anyway, Lazarus liked Elias's company. The old man was not big on small talk. Although when he had some beer or cheap brandy in him he could spin a yarn or two.

Elias was not frightened by Lazarus's prison tattoos. He had faced the gunfire of the South African Defence Force in the jungles of Angola and the rolling Casspirs and the sjamboks of the koevoets in the North. In his sleep he still heard the bombs as they dropped on Cassinga. Sometimes his slumber would be fitful, and he would whimper until Lazarus shook him awake.

The two men regarded each other as equals, both outcast by their former allegiances. Lazarus never volunteered information about his prison stint. Elias never asked. Everyone brought a past to the street and the present was always hungry. The street snacked on those who regretted, those who dreamt of a tomorrow that still required today to be survived.

That was the first thing Elias told Lazarus: the street has no future, there is only today. And today you need food. Today you need shelter. Today you need to take care of today.

On garbage days the two would methodically scour every bin they could find in their old territories of Katutura, Hakahana, Goreangab, Wanaheda and Okuryangava. But poor people's bins are slim pickings, and Elias and Lazarus talk about those days learnedly, trying to pass on what they know to Martin, Silas and Omagano.

'When we started out, we weren't picky. We had to survive,' Elias says.

'When you have to survive you don't get to choose what you have to do,' Lazarus trails.

'Everywhere, we went. Everything, we did.'

'We had to survive, *julle ken*.'

'But you can't survive by being around people who are also trying to survive,' Elias continues. 'All you'll get is whatever they don't need to survive, you see?'

'You need to go where people have enough to throw away.'

'Where there are white people.'

Lazarus laughs a little. 'Or black people trying to be white people.'

'Then you can survive there.'

'Remember when we found the baby?' Lazarus asks. This is a common evening tale. 'That was when we knew we had to upgrade.'

'We are going through the bins. In neighbourhoods where we even have cousins, aunts and uncles. In places where people might know us. But we go through them.'

'To survive, *mos*, just to survive.'

Elias's voice becomes grave. 'Usually in a bin you have to be ready to find shit. Old food, used condoms, women's things with blood on them, broken things. Those things are fine. When things don't have a use they get thrown away, neh? But this time we are in a big bin by the side of the road. I reach for some newspapers I see so we can start a fire that night. They are wrapped around something and I lift it up. When I open it I scream and I run.'

'I think he has found a snake the way he runs,' Lazarus chuckles, a haw-haw sound like a saw biting into a thick piece of wood. Then he becomes quiet. 'But I see in the newspapers the baby *met sy umbilliese koord toegedraai om sy nek. Jirre jisses!* I also ran.'

'Dead dog? It is okay,' Elias says. 'Dead cat? It is okay. It is witchcraft. Cats is witchcraft.'

Omagano nods her agreement. 'Even dead

person is also okay.' Martin's face shows his shock and revulsion and that makes Silas laugh. He really is new to the streets. 'People die, *laaitie*. Or maybe the dead person thought he was smart and said something foolish and now he is not going to say anything foolish ever again. Dead person is okay. But dead baby? That is something else.'

'Dead baby is evil,' Lazarus says. Omagano wraps her arms underneath her breasts and rocks herself a little.

'So,' Elias says after a while, 'we get smart. We move away from poor people. We find a flyer from the municipality with all of the rubbish collection dates. We make a timetable and we start watching the neighbourhoods even before there is a neighbourhood watch.'

'On Tuesday and Thursday nights we stop going to poor people's places because poor people have nothing left to throw away but themselves.'

Wednesdays, In Days Past: Khomasdal
There are some neighbourhoods not worth fighting over. Dorado Park and Khomasdal are crowded with other starving, roving cliques. The neighbourhoods are already spoken for. All the places that break the wind have long-term tenants and all the generous churches already have their squabbling regulars. The Neighbourhood Watch never enters Khomasdal because people drink too much there. Alcohol is what took Amos. Not really. It was pride.

After a particularly good week, Elias, Lazarus and Amos decided to water their throats at one of the many bottle stores that siphon husbands away from their wives and families on Friday and Saturday nights. They shared three quarts of Zamalek to start, then a cheap whisky, then some more beer. If there were two things Amos could never hold it was his tongue and his drink. But it was his tongue that carried more consequences. It was his tongue that cursed people with swear words that could scour the grime and funk off a dirty pavement. It was his tongue that goaded people on. It was his tongue that called someone a *ma se poes*. That same tongue refused to apologize for the slight. Amos could never bring himself to back down from anything.

Then there were three things Amos could not hold. His tongue, his drink and his guts.

The knife flashed quickly. In, out, in, out, and then slashed across.

Amos looked at his bloody hands and tottered on the spot.

Before the fall comes...

Amos fell.

Everyone ran.

If there is one thing that is bad for everyone on the streets, friend or foe, temporarily homeless or permanently on the pavement, it is a dead body.

A dead body has to be explained. To the police. Who like their explanations to be delivered quickly. Slow explanations can be sped up by a few baton bashes in the back of a police van. By the time they throw someone in the holding cell half the crime has already been solved. The paperwork is what seems to frustrate them the most.

That is why everyone ran. Even Elias and Lazarus.

Especially Elias and Lazarus.

The first thing the police do is look for the dead body's living pals. They ask questions. Hard, booted questions. If they know someone is innocent, they kick harder. But if someone has the good sense to be guilty they ease up because nobody wants the magistrate to ask questions about cuts, bruises and bumps. Sometimes, when there has been a spate of robberies or a murder the police cannot close quickly enough, they come around and ask someone to take the fall. Jail has food and shelter and sometimes that looks like a good deal. If it is a murder that has made headlines they will offer even better conditions. A single cell, maybe more food. Maybe put you in the same block as a friend. Sometimes someone takes the offer. The streets are not for everyone.

Elias and Lazarus ran until their lungs gave out and then they continued on.

When the police finally caught up with Elias and Lazarus they were interrogated roughly at first and then they were questioned politely. Elias said polite questioning was the worst thing he had ever endured. Worse, even, than being beaten for days on end when he was caught by the boers during the insurgency years.

They were eventually let go because they refused to change their story. Yes, they were there when Amos was stabbed. They ran because they were afraid. No, they did not do it. No, they would not say that they did it. No, they did not see who did it. No, they could not identify anyone if they were shown pictures.

Could they then, to a reasonable degree – and, of course, a bruised, bleeding degree – be certain that they had not, in fact, murdered Amos for 200 dollars and then run away after ditching the bloody knife that lay on the table in front of them? Yes, they could be.

For their reasonableness they were let go with a warning, swollen eyes, three broken ribs a pair, and limps that took days to heal – a bargain, really, all things considered. Bones heal, cuts stop bleeding. Everything grows over or grows back, except life.

Elias and Lazarus were lucky. But they chose not to go back to Khomasdal in case the man who killed Amos thought they were out for retribution.

Friday and Saturday: Headquarters
Under the bridge, behind some bushes, away from the others, Omagano lays down. First Elias takes his turn and then when he is finished Lazarus waits for Omagano to call him so he can also take his. Omagano is only for Elias and Lazarus. Silas

and Martin are not allowed to touch her under any circumstances. They are told they are too young. Omagano looks at them with scorn when they make indecent proposals to her.

Instead Silas and Martin have to make the spit. Silas shows Martin how.

Martin has to pull down his dirty denims to his ankles and bring his legs together. Silas spits on his thighs and spreads the saliva between them. Then Martin has to lie on his side while Silas lies behind him thrusting into the friction until he is finished. Martin rolls over and wipes his thighs and asks Silas to do the same. Silas refuses. It is Martin's job as a new member to make the spit. Silas had to do it when it was just Elias, Lazarus and him. Then Omagano joined and the two men claimed her. For now, it is Martin's turn to make the spit for Silas, and for Elias and for Lazarus when Omagano is going through her woman phases. Maybe if they find a younger girl to join then Martin will not have to make the spit. Or maybe Elias and Lazarus will take the younger girl and give them Omagano. She will be old. But an older woman is better than making the spit.

Fridays and Saturdays are generally spent under the bridge at Headquarters. Elias calls it that because he used to be in the Struggle. He calls broken bottles and thorns APMs. When someone has a wound that needs to be looked at he says it is time for a Tampax Tiffie and when they are low on food he says it is time for the rats.

Headquarters is a safer place to be on Fridays and Saturdays because those are the days when the police drive around looking for any signs of mischief. They are the days when pride is most likely to manifest itself. Amos died on a Friday night.

Silas cannot resist leaving Headquarters though. He calls to Martin to join him but Lazarus says no. Martin cannot go. If Silas is going he must go by himself. If mischief finds him he must know no one will come to look for him.

Elias, Lazarus, Omagano and Martin sit at Headquarters and talk about what they saw in the streets that day. They talk about the fools who sit by the roadside in Klein Windhoek and Eros, hoping they can paint a room, fix a window, install a sink, or lay some tiles.

'They are too proud to be like us,' Elias says. 'But they are the ones going home hungry every day.'

'Pride is poor food,' Lazarus says.

'But sometimes they can find a job,' Martin chirps.

'They can, sometimes,' Elias answers. 'But they can find a job as often as we can find 20,000 dollars. How many times have we found 20,000 dollars?'

Martin's brow furrows as he thinks and that makes Lazarus laugh. 'Idiot,' he says.

'Maybe things can get better for them,' Martin says.

Elias and Lazarus look at him and then at each other. They sense hope, the spoor that leads the street to your hiding place. 'Maybe is tomorrow, *laaitie*,' Lazarus says.

'And there is only today,' Elias adds.

'Today you need food. Today you need shelter. Today you need to take care of today.'

'And tomorrow?' Martin asks. Omagano harrumphs.

'Every day is today,' Elias says.

Sunday: Avis, Klein Windhoek and Eros

Sundays are the best days. Eros and Klein Windhoek have the highest walls, dogs safely penned behind fences, bins lined up on the pavement, and, most importantly, people who recycle. The paper, cardboard, plastic bottles, tin cans and aluminium foil are sorted into separate plastic bags. Some people even wash the trash before they throw it away. Everything else that is of no use goes in the big green bins, which is a much more efficient way to forage. It saves time, mitigates disappointment. Those suburbs are also close to Headquarters, so the Neighbourhood Watch does not have to stray too far from their home.

The best thing about Eros is old Mrs Bezuidenhout. She sits on her front porch in the early evening with her son, waiting for the Neighbourhood Watch to come by. When she sees them wheeling their trolley down her street she calls to them. They pause by her gate as she goes into her house. They wait while she makes her slow, brittle way to the electric gate, cheeks sucking in and out on her gums, her son watching her every step. Her gate slides open a fraction and she hands them a plastic bag. Some cans of beans and peas, two or three bananas. She gave them the pair of scissors they use to cut their hair. She gave them the circle of mirror that shames their appearance on some days. In winter she collects old clothes and knits jerseys or blankets from an endless supply of wool. She hands them old books, which they burn, and rosaries they read with their fingers in the dead of night when only God and the streets listen.

The Neighbourhood Watch has three pillars: Elias's street savoir-faire, Lazarus's contained violence and Mrs Bezuidenhout's generosity. For her, the Neighbourhood Watch would fight all of the gangs of Windhoek if they had to. Lazarus is not a believer but even he says Mrs Bezuiden-hout is worth praying for, and to. When she sees them she asks them how they are. Elias replies for them. '*Ons is okay, Mevrou Bezuidenhout.*' She asks them if they need anything else. '*Niks, ons het net nodig wat jy vir ons gegee het.*'

Silas once asked Elias why he never asked for toothbrushes, or soap, or medicine, or a space in her garage where they could sleep, if she was being so generous. Elias said it was because Mrs Bezuidenhout took from them more than she gave. 'She gives and she gives and we take and we take. Soon she will not be around to give and give but we will still need to take and take. She gives something from her home to us and takes some of the street away from us. We need all of the street to survive the street. You understand now?'

The Neighbourhood Watch starts in Avis as the sun is setting, hunting for the new apartment complexes that bring a fresh crop of bins to the interlocked pavements, shying away from joggers who avert their eyes when they see them and dog walkers who slacken their grips on leashes. Then they traverse the steep hills of Klein Windhoek where people only put out their bins at the crack of dawn to dissuade the dustbin divers from perambulating through their streets. That is how bad it has become, Lazarus says. The rich have got so rich they have started hoarding their trash. From there they scour Eros, from top to bottom, through all the streets named after mountains they will never climb, the rivers they shall never see, all the precious stones they will never hold: Everest, Atlas and the Drakensberg; Orange, Kunene, Okavango and Kuiseb; Amethyst, Topaz and Tourmaline. They rove and roam across the neighbourhood like wildebeest following the rains, the street following them like a hungry predator.

They leave Mrs Bezuidenhout's street for last, eager for her kindness, afraid of the day when she will no longer be around to give and give, when they will still need to take and take, when there will not be enough street in them to face the street. The day before they hit Eros, the day before they visit Mrs Bezuidenhout, the Neighbourhood Watch break their one rule. They start thinking of the day that is not today, they say goodbye to the day that is yesterday, and worse, they start thinking of the day that is tomorrow.

Rémy Ngamije is a Rwandan-born Namibian writer and photographer. His debut novel *The Eternal Audience Of One* is forthcoming from Scout Press (S&S). He is the editor-in-chief of *Doek!*, Namibia's first literary magazine. His short stories have appeared in *Litro Magazine*, *AFREADA*, *Johannesburg Review of Books*, *The Amistad*, *Kalahari Review*, *American Chordata*, *Doek!*, *Azure*, *Sultan's Seal*, *Santa Ana River Review*, *Columbia Journal*, *New Contrast*, *Necessary Fiction*, *Silver Pinion* and *Lolwe*. He has been longlisted for the 2020 Afritondo Short Story Prize and shortlisted for Best Original Fiction by Stack Magazines in 2019. 'The Neighbourhood Watch' was first published in *The Johannesburg Review of Books* in 2019.
www.remythequill.com Twitter: @remythequill

stomach, acid eroding the words into nothing. She could shit it out. Could you shit out paper? That would particularly encapsulate what it was: ugly. Or she could simply misplace it in the flat somewhere. Not outside. Definitely not outside. It would be gone for ever then. She'd have to go through options again, add new ones, whittle it down. That process had left her brain frazzled overnight, her heart leaking through the bedroom keyhole, making a sucking sound as her hands turned to wax. The receipt would have to be misplaced indoors. That would give her the option of attempting to stretch the boundaries of time despite an internal wound the shape of a turret.

In her mind, the draughtsman was God. He had placed the turret inside her chest. Earlier, he'd drawn her in various angles, electric blue lines delivering degrees of shock from the same incident. Each time she got up. Each time she felt the weight of the turret tumbling in the ether.

She picked up the receiver, cradled it firmly, careful not to let it slip from her grasp the way things had of late. For a few seconds there was silence at the other end. She knew it was Hassan. He usually waited several beats before speaking, as if allowing you time to adjust to a different frequency. He never introduced himself. He just expected you to know. And she always did.

Sidra, so there's a party tonight. You don't have to attend, might be fun, though. The guy's a big Grace Jones fan. I've texted you the address. Do what you do. Any problems, call me. Cool?

Bet.

She almost told him about the draughtsman then. She found herself wanting to do it at the most unexpected times. Instead she put the receiver down, hands trembling. She checked the table for the receipt. It had fallen onto the floor by the radiator, already misplacing itself. She'd forgotten to tell Hassan that she was considering taking an evening class one day a week. They were like that, so many things constantly left unsaid. She'd never asked him what a French-Algerian man was doing running a lookalike agency in London among other things. And he'd never asked what a girl from Martinique with a degree in forensics was doing moonlighting as a Grace Jones impersonator, the translated versions of themselves staring at each other silently from the opposite sides of a revolving door.

* * *

There was a building that remained a husk; a blackened, charcoaled carcass gutted from the inside out. The carcass leaned against the heavens in protest at its losses, at its snatched internal sky tainted with the fingerprints of one last daily procession, rituals of the living. And while the world slept, awoke, the cities hummed with chaos and order; rivers began in cotton pockets cupping slackened fists; the waters undulated into lost reflections; the gods got high off the colours from the seas; the equator adjusted itself only slightly; the stars twinkled in haphazard collusion; the mountains dappled by Harmattan winds that became personal directions; the building remained, an artificial gut bathed in degrees of light, lodged in the stages of a day. The building was a hollow within a carcass within a husk within a world within a galaxy; a series of crooked boxes varying in size inside each other where the gift was always the same, always attached to a bottom that had gone missing. On each floor of the husk, Sidra was running backwards to the late afternoon of a day. It had been flat-packed into cardboard boxes sealed with Sellotape. On each floor Sidra peeled off the Sellotape, the sound a split in the air whose line couldn't be traced. She removed items from the box. The late afternoon that day was made up of ingredients for cake: eggs, flour, butter, sugar, tinfoil, a whisk, vanilla.

On each floor Sidra ran to the window where she stood in costumes made of tinfoil.

On floor one she was covered with eggs, screaming.

On floor two she was drenched in flour, howling.

On floor three she was soaked in butter, melting as a heat intensified while the whisk whirred ominously on the periphery.

And so on.

Grace Jones's 'La Vie en Rose' played on a radio that wasn't plugged in anywhere. Instead the plug sprang from the bottom of the building, like an untethered electrical root.

The husk shook.

On each floor Sidra grabbed the whisk. Lost scenes fell out from the windows; water was inadequate. Hoses throbbed with adrenalin and burned hearts; death traps, the lifts became stuck all over again spewing firefighters' costumes like overgrown fabricated insects. Like genesis on speed, everything escalated quickly. Ashes assembled into figures crawling on the skyline before colliding with traffic, which destroyed them all over again.

The equator turned a fraction.

The flames rose.

The bottoms of the crooked boxes were set alight.

Debris became glowing cinders that walked.

A dot appeared on the galaxy.

The draughtsman held a flame he angled like a stick of lead, like a tool that could change guise at any point.

* * *

Sidra had first seen Grace on TV. She must have been around thirteen at the time. She'd been chasing Carla and Dorian, who were playing with a set of screwdrivers behind the sofa, darting forwards and backwards in a mock game of fencing, shouting 'En garde!' sporadically, brandishing the screwdrivers like long, elegantly carved swords. The washing-machine was spinning. The windows were open to hide evidence of her botched attempt at gumbo. The smoke alarm was broken. Half an hour earlier, it had beeped incessantly. In her frustrated efforts to silence it, she'd broken it with a broom. But none of that mattered because a woman who looked like her was on TV. Pulled to the screen by an instinct she didn't quite understand, she stared. It was on BBC1. She'd never seen a black woman so unapologetically dark on the screen. It was beautiful and she was hypnotized. Dressed in an all-black cat suit, the woman was tall, striking, other-worldly, confident.

Her mouth painted fire-engine red, her head was in an off-yellow helmet shaped like a bees' nest. Sidra half expected a swarm of bees to hover over the woman's head, the queen bee in action. She felt as if they'd shared the same womb, separated by a few decades and a trail of bees' fat with mutual DNA and womb lining.

Grace Jones, they said. Grace Jones.

She repeated the words aloud, feeling them roll off her tongue while the washing-machine spun, while Carla and Dorian swapped the screwdrivers for Power Ranger toys starting wars in patois. The screen jumped, flickered, the picture vanished.

Grace had been brought to her on a signal from Jupiter.

She grabbed the hanger on the floor behind the TV, stretched its curved head and inserted it into the television's aerial socket. The picture returned. Grace was gone, replaced by an item on an infected brand of milk. Her heart sank but the image of Grace was burned into her head as if with an iron. She ran to her mother's room, opened her make-up drawers searching through the lipsticks, pouting her lips. She flung the wardrobe door open, its mirrors multiplying her automatically. She dived in. In the dark, she heard the flutter of a wing. A bee with a fire-engine-red mouth floated in a trail of static.

* * *

Sidra hopped into a cab to East Dulwich, the Roland Mouret jacket shimmering in the cold night. Her Yves St Laurent perfume mingled with a scent that smelt oddly like pot-pourri. Her red velvet backless cat suit was warm and luxurious against her skin. In the back seat, she could make out the top of her face in the rear-view mirror: short back and sides, no fuss, good to go. Dangling from the mirror was a miniature golden Aladdin-esque lamp. She sank into the seat as the city unfolded, fingers tracing the possibilities of the inky darkness, picturing the lamp spilling petrol into the hemline of a dress she'd decided not to wear. She rolled the window down as the driver talked non-stop about being a boy in Damascus.

The cool breeze pricked her skin. She closed her eyes, the driver's ramblings seeping in almost subconsciously.

She hadn't been to East Dulwich for a few years. Not since she'd worked for a mobile massage company for one week. That first job, she'd found a slender, bespectacled man of average height sprinkling the green outside a large house in a silk kimono-style dressing-gown. He adjusted the wire-rimmed glasses perched on his nose inter-mittently as if out of habit. The house was like something from *Wallpaper* magazine: futuristic, slightly incongruous in that leafy, suburban street. He abandoned the sprinkler, pleased at the sight of her, motioned towards the open front door. They walked in. In the hallway, he disappeared for roughly a minute, then reappeared holding a towel. He handed her the towel, instructing her to change in the downstairs bathroom ahead, £150 for a topless 40-minute massage. She got ready. Dressed in black panties, netted stockings, suspenders and a silver cape, she climbed the stairs where she found him in a neon wrestling outfit in the master bedroom, a pot of cream standing on a lovingly crafted small bedside table. They wrestled for ten minutes. Then she smeared the cream on his face, yanking his head down into the puddle of white on the wooden floor, forcing him to lick it.

Afterwards, stripped down on the bed, the light fracturing on the chandelier, she kneaded his hairy back. He groaned, complimenting the warmth of her hands.

The fire for him started in the bathroom with the draughtsman sitting at the edge of the tub wearing her silver cape, smiling encouragingly.

That week, the fires began in a different room each time: a basement, a study, a conservatory. Sidra would always remember that first one: the silken kimono flapping open to reveal an expanse of thigh, a line of hair creeping into his groin, the cuckoo clock with a tiny woman whose arms were the hands of time, whose cuckooing mouth was decorated with soot that would spread, the irony of the sprinkler still turning on the green as she left, watering kernels of afternoon secrets before lapsing into silence.

* * *

The cab pulled up to a Georgian mansion. Sidra paid, tipping the driver an extra ten pounds for his stories. She jumped out, crossing the large stretch of lawn dotted with pale tents draped with flickering lights, a hedge carved into the shape of a figure holding a chainsaw and a life-sized family of ice swans craning their necks towards each other, slowly thawing into the grass. She knocked on the door. A Marilyn Monroe lookalike opened it, appropriately dressed in a bombshell blue polka-dot Sixties dress.

'Welcome!' she announced theatrically. 'You

look fabulous,' she added, stepping aside to allow Sidra entrance.

The waft of warm air smelt like expensive aftershaves, mince pies, perfume. The décor was classily understated, with colourful touches here and there. Sidra raised her head. There were three floors, from what she could see. Bodies everywhere, jostling, sliding and wriggling through as if they'd been let out of giant tin cans slick and oiled in some saccharine sheen for excess, the sharp, opened-can ceilings edging closely to their foreheads as they moved. She took off her jacket, slipping it over her arm as a Rod Stewart lookalike approached, offering to take it. She declined, looking beyond him to a tray of hors d'oeuvres being served by a Pee-wee Herman lookalike in a grey suit, white brogues, topped off with a red bow tie. She assessed the guests. There were no other black people. She wasn't planning on serving any hors d'oeuvres. Fuck that shit. She was used to being the only black female lookalike at this sort of gathering unless Tina Turner showed up, cutting her out of oxygen and attention. Tina wasn't there. Thank God. Marilyn Monroe had smoothly grabbed her a glass of white wine. She took the hollow-stemmed flute.

'You look so much like her,' Sidra said, offering what every impersonator wanted to hear.

Marilyn blushed. 'My heart just jumped with joy,' she answered breathlessly, in a perfect impersonation of her idol. 'Luigi's just through in the other room.'

Sidra followed the sound of the piano to Luigi, their host, a squat, balding, jewelled, enthusiastic film producer, who made the phrase 'larger than life' inadequate in his presence. Celebrating his annual end-of-year soirée, he sat before a sleek black piano, flanked by three Venuses feeding him miniature salmon slices topped with cream on tiny puffs of pastry. Delighted, Luigi pointed at her. 'Pull up to my bumper, baby!' He bashed the piano keys dramatically.

A crowd circled her. Sidra tugged her handbag strap up her shoulder. The small crowd were gasping, barely restraining themselves from reaching out to touch her, chattering over each other.

She smiled at this part of what was essentially a ceremony, a performance. This part always felt good. The bodies leaned in, clutching their wine glasses. The draughtsman appeared behind them holding two yellow-handled screwdrivers. There were tongues in the wine flutes, floating, then curling mid-scream, sinking to the bottom. Sidra closed her eyes momentarily as the humming in her brain began. She disappeared into her role: Grace Jones.

* * *

Several months back, there'd been another party, a masked ball in Paris in a former museum on the border of the Champs-Élysées. There on business, Hassan had informed her he might or might not attend. He was elusive that way. She never knew when he'd turn up to keep a distant but watchful eye on events. As the owner of the agency he didn't need to; occasionally he materialized to keep his band of impersonators on their toes.

She'd left the mingling crowds, making her way through a maze of decadent rooms until she entered one right at the back of the building. Original surrealist paintings hung on the walls, tanks full of moon starfish slowly pulsed rhythmically in calm, contained, lit waters. A deep Egyptian gold-trimmed coffin lay open. She'd been running her fingers over the trimming when she felt a hand on her back, a finger slowly circling. Something about that touch felt familiar. She leaned into it, ill-equipped to resist an unspooling occurring in her stomach.

'Hassan?' She turned around. The man didn't speak. He wore an intricately designed silver mask. There was no way to make out his face. Dressed in an exquisitely tailored midnight-blue suit, which complemented his skin tone, he reminded her of Hassan. He was similar in height, stature, tall and lean, possibly Arab. He had the same unruly head of curly hair. A smell like Cuban cigars and spirit-lined edges emanated from him. He possessed the same amused glint in his eyes. Instead of answering her, he took her hand, led her into the silk-lined coffin. He reached under her bulbous terracotta-coloured ballgown skirt, took off her panties. He parted her arse, burying his tongue there, licking and sucking greedily, groaning as his tongue circled, darted and fucked her rectum as though it was an edible orchid. He fucked her in that coffin without taking off a stitch of clothing. They were realigned, cushioned by folds of material. Sidra revealed her secret as she came, unable to understand how it had emerged from a burrow within her. He didn't react, as if he hadn't heard her. Stepping out of the coffin, their silence was a shared language. He kissed her neck tenderly before leaving. The moon starfish exited their tanks, floated towards her, running out of time.

Back in the main space, she scanned the crowds dribbling in different directions. He'd vanished. She headed outside to catch her breath in the courtyard. The moon starfish became mushrooms falling from her skin.

* * *

Three weeks later in London, Hassan invited her to a working-lunch meeting. He was immaculate, of course, in a teak-coloured Ozwald Boateng blazer, black polo neck and slacks. He had a way of making instructions sound like casual suggestions, though with an undertone that made it clear he was absolutely serious. In between his briefing, she caught an unexpected expression on his face.

She'd been reaching into her purse to pay half of the bill. He was watching her as if he knew her intimately. It was a warm, mischievous look, so fleeting that afterwards she thought she'd imagined it. Then his eyes became hooded, his expression darkened.

'It's an easy gig. No matter how inebriated you get, avoid leaving with anybody you don't know. I don't want a fucking heart attack in my mid-thirties. And stay away from stuff with traces of peanut. You're allergic. Remember that time your face swelled up? You looked like the Elephant Woman.' He chuckled.

Sidra cringed internally at the memory. Of course he'd remember that embarrassing incident. He told her about his trip to Greece, his work providing for and co-ordinating the refugee relief there. He spoke passionately at some length, fondly relaying amusing tales of some of the characters he'd encountered, the children in particular, how crazy the camps were, the cama-raderie formed despite the desperation of their situation. She hadn't expected that level of gener-osity from him. The truth was, she knew very little about him beyond their working relation-ship. She suspected even his occasional revela-tions were calculated, though she was unsure as to what end.

'Is there something you'd like to tell me?' he

'Hope we're having more than cake for dinner,' she said, smiling, before peeling off her nursing uniform then crawling into bed. At the kitchen table, Sidra scribbled down a brief list. They'd run out of vanilla extract, the flour wasn't enough, no icing sugar left. She slipped on her jacket, trainers. She double-locked the flat door with her keys, as she often did if she needed to pop out, briefly leaving her siblings alone. The lift smelt of piss and sweat, groaning all the way down fourteen floors, shuddering as if it would spit her out onto an exit beyond the confines of the building. She departed it, remembering she'd knocked the roll of tinfoil onto the kitchen floor, left the fridge and cupboard doors open, Carla and Dorian arguing about a broken toy plane. She'd recall those details later. She'd weigh them in her hands, wrap them in tinfoil, pass them through the expanding hole in her chest, watching their arrival on a periphery, bloody, misshapen, despite their thin veil of protection.

It was the vanilla extract that delayed her. They'd run out of it practically everywhere in their area. She'd had to walk all the way down to the cash-and-carry at the end of the main road to find a bottle. Forty minutes was all it took to lose everything. She arrived back to find their block engulfed in flames. The fire was ferocious. People jumped out of windows from the lower floors; babies were thrown out in duvets; bedsheets were used as inadequate ropes. The popping of fire, the screams of panic strangled her internally. She spilled the shopping on the horizon, the icing darkened by a trail of soot, the vanilla bottle breathing smoke, the flour dousing trees, windows, hands on car wheels steering, fingers jamming in ignitions instead of keys. It didn't matter which element of the scene she stumbled on unexpectedly, her mother, Carla and Dorian were trapped. The fire raged on. Her brother and sister died in their mother's arms. Powerless, Sidra had stood on the pavement looking up, screaming, a chipped chess piece floundering between the firefighters, hoses, the crowd. She'd locked her family in to protect them. She'd locked her family in, killing them.

The parts of that memory always assembled into the same inevitable ending.

She'd brought out the keys, her hands shaking uncontrollably, her mouth babbling mother, cake, fridge, lift, uniform.

She tried inserting the keys inside their names as if they were locks that would open, materialize them in her arms so she could breathe again. Instead the keys stuck, refusing to turn. They jammed in every opening, every possibility of rescue. In the years that were to follow, Sidra would encounter her actions that day again and again. And the draughtsman started appearing.

* * *

The party continued, a barely contained beast sprouting various heads while the skyline unfurled. Pee-wee Herman knelt in the garden doorway drinking Dom Pérignon from another man's shoes. Luigi had disappeared from his own celebration. A silver-haired contortionist lay sprawled atop the piano, twisting, then curling her body into astonishing shapes as bright ties spilled from her mouth. People were doing lines of coke on the staircase, in the toilets, on the pantry floor. In the ground-floor bathroom there were bodies in the tub, clothed mannequins blinking at the harsh light, knocked out by their debauchery and excess. There were people fucking in the tents on the lawn, the cold air mottling their skin, the small decorative lights jangling as if indicating the tents might collapse, folding into bodies as part of the thrill.

Inside the kitchen, Sidra thought about the sharp instruments that found their way into the margins of her life, how they blunted against her body. She reached for a plum from a bowl of fruit on the grey marble island top. Instead of cores, in her mind's eye the fruit had miniature blackened vanilla-extract bottles spilling elixir for multiple deaths. She held up the plum. The draughtsman took a bite. She glanced at the hallway. There were bodies all the way up the banister shedding alligator skin, mouths holding their vices between knocked-out teeth, feet leaking watery reflections. The draughtsman finished the plum. Sidra took another swig of wine, looked up at the patterns of swirls on the white ceiling, longing for some entity to pull her through rust, wood, metal, bone, perform an excavation that would leave her changed. She felt hollow, gutted. She'd become acclimatized to scenes of this nature, adjusting herself in degrees, like a heating dial.

* * *

Before the tower block became a burned husk there stood an old print house in its place. Before the print house there were raw materials to build it. Before those raw materials there was a draughtsman named Alrik, armed with a vision. Before the vision there was a perilous journey crossing the Atlantic Ocean to England by ship. Alrik had left behind a young son and a spirited wife, whose plans to join him in London spurred him on while he searched for work. But his wife and son died of cholera making that same journey, which for him had been loaded with hunger, curiosity and wonder at the potential of his new life. Their bodies were flung into the cold, thrashing sea.

Broken-hearted and forlorn, Alrik spent time numbing his loss in the opium dens of London. It was in one such den that the image of the print house came to him, a building where men printed endless trails of paper, a building topped off with a turret, a kind of signature, a reference to his travels beyond the Americas. The image was ingrained in his memory that night at the den in Limehouse, floating alluringly between curls of smoke.

Roughly a month later, Alrik got himself a job at a construction company. He worked his way up. By the time the print house was built in 1920, he'd married a grocer's daughter named Bethany. They had three sons. He went on to draft designs for other projects but the print house remained his favourite because it came to him during a period of great pain, its lines somehow made indelible in his bloodstream, constructed in memory of his first wife and son.

Before he died, Alrik was grateful the building would outlive him. In 1970, his beautiful print house was knocked down, having been a barely used museum for years, and replaced by an ugly tower block of flats. Resurrected from the rubble, Alrik began to wander through the tower block regularly. He entered people's flats, breathed against oven doors, sources of electricity. He searched for his departed reflection in their mirrors. Resentful, angry, he set small accidents for which occupants would absentmindedly feel responsible. Dissatisfied, over the years he began to plot a bigger accident worthy of his loss. At first, he simply fiddled with the wiring of the building, ensured the lifts malfunctioned now and again, and removed the fire extinguishers. Over time, his acts of malice grew. The draughtsman cultivated his appetite for destruction.

* * *

Sidra had met the real Grace Jones once after her concert at the Royal Albert Hall, for which Grace had been fashionably an hour late. She'd cornered her at the end by the backstage entrance, fighting through other bodies jostling to do the same.

'Grace!' she'd hollered, overwhelmed by excitement. 'People tell me I remind them of you.'

Grace, decked in a tight see-through chiffon dress, purple knee-length boots and white 3D glasses had smiled patiently, tolerantly. 'Dahhhling, imitation is for pagans but you are divine.'

Sidra found Luigi strangling one of the Venuses in the secret garden behind an initial smaller, more standard-looking garden. It ran lengthways. Venus was so out of it, she could barely fight back or scream. Her feet kicked limply. Her soiled, sequined dress's train was a fish tail moored on the wrong Garden of Eden. A little unsteadily, Sidra set her jacket down. She leaped onto Luigi pummelling his back. 'Leave her alone!' Venus's underwear was gone; there were bruises already forming on her thighs. For a rotund, shorter man, Luigi, was surprisingly strong. Barely recognizable as the charming host she'd encountered several hours earlier, he wore a chilling, cold expression. 'Fuck off, you cunt.' Turning around, he punched Sidra in the face repeatedly. Venus stared blankly at a night sky that wouldn't rescue her. Sidra fell backwards. The wind left her body. Her head spun; her handbag went flying. She felt the weight of the perfume bottle slide as it moved. Blood trickled from her nose into her mouth. Her face throbbed. She looked at her Roland Mouret jacket, half expecting it to morph into a parachute, a dizzying, shimmering distraction from the ache in her head, which felt like it would fracture. Then there were four other Grace Jones lookalikes dressed exactly like her. They all reached for her purse, for an item that accompanied her constantly: petrol in a perfume bottle, a beating heart liquefied.

The draughtsman resurfaced and all his fingers were flames.

The fire at Luigi's was voracious. Just like all the others. It swallowed the once-glorious building, tore through the roof. It puffed black smoke, spat screaming bodies out. On the front lawn, Sidra coughed from the smoke in her lungs. Luigi, engulfed in flames, ran erratically, a wind-up life-sized toy, attempting to put himself out.

The pale tents empty of bodies were on fire; the ice swans' heads had melted, the remains of their figures thinning mockingly; the giant hedge man had lost his chainsaw.

Ambulance and fire-engine sirens screamed in the distance.

A familiar figure ran towards her. Hassan. He looked dishevelled, half panicked, a tight expression on his face. This man who was always cool, calm and assured grabbed her in relief. 'Thank God! This was on the news. I was out of my mind with worry. You're going to give me internal injuries before I hit forty.' He cupped her battered face. 'Who did this? I'll kill him.'

She tried to speak but couldn't. What she wanted to say was: couldn't somebody hear her silently screaming inside for years? Couldn't somebody in this fucking world get their hands bloody reaching into her guts to find something jagged and beautiful she could hold up to the light?

Couldn't somebody see that she disappeared into Grace Jones because the pain, the guilt, the loneliness of being herself was unbearable? Couldn't somebody remind her of her favourite thing about being alive since she'd forgotten? Couldn't somebody find the bright yolk she'd lost in the back of a cab on a rainy afternoon, then present it to her as a new beginning? Couldn't somebody just be tender? She stuck her hand into her jacket pocket. A receipt poked out; it fell. She hadn't remembered slipping it in there but she must have done. Miraculously, it had survived the fire. She'd taken the inside creature outside, disguised as a creased receipt. She wondered if it would anger the draughtsman.

Hassan held the receipt, gazing at the three options she'd written down. Shaken, he stared as if holding a grenade pin with the world attached to it. He ripped up the receipt, its pieces fluttering in the cold air as the fire raged behind them.

'When you're ready, tell me what you've been scared to say,' he suggested. She started crying then. He held her, pressed his mouth against the pulse in her neck as if it was a light travelling, as if it would be mercury by the time he finished knowing it. He held onto her. They braced themselves for the weather in the cracks, for the draughtsman's next stroke.

Irenosen Okojie is a Nigerian-British writer. Her debut novel *Butterfly Fish* won a Betty Trask award and was shortlisted for an Edinburgh International First Book Award. Her work has been featured in the *New York Times*, *The Observer*, *The Guardian*, the BBC and the *Huffington Post* amongst other publications. Her short stories have been published internationally, including in *Salt's Best British Short Stories 2017, Kwani?* and *The Year's Best Weird Fiction*. She was presented at the London Short Story Festival by Booker Prize-winning author Ben Okri as a dynamic writing talent to watch and featured in the *Evening Standard Magazine* as one of London's exciting new authors. Her short story collection *Speak Gigantular*, published by Jacaranda Books, was shortlisted for the Edgehill Short Story Prize, the Jhalak Prize, the Saboteur Awards and nominated for a Shirley Jackson Award. She is a fellow of the Royal Society of Literature. Her new collection of stories, *Nudibranch*, is published by Little Brown's Dialogue Books and 'Grace Jones' first appeared in that book.

www.irenosenokojie.com Twitter: @IrenosenOkojie

Support literary and cultural excellence from Africa through the Caine Prize for African Writing

"Over the years, the Caine Prize has done a great deal to foster writing in Africa and bring exciting new African writers to the attention of wider audiences"

J.M. Coetzee, Nobel Prize Laureate for Literature

About Us

The Caine Prize for African Writing was launched in 2000 with the aim of encouraging and highlighting the rich diversity of African writing by bringing it to a wider, international audience. The prize is named after the late Sir Michael Caine, Chairman of the 'Africa 95' arts festival in Europe and Africa in 1995 and for nearly 25 years Chairman of the Booker Prize management committee. We are a registered charity whose aim is to bring African writing to a wider audience using our annual literary award. We do not benefit from an endowment and rely on raising funds to continue our work each year. We are passionate and committed to seeing Africa's stories told in all their nuance and complexity and welcome your support of our mission.

HOW TO GIVE

To find out more about how to give please visit:
www.caineprize.com/donate

If you would like to enquire about sponsorship and partnership with the Caine Prize, please email:
info@caineprize.com

The AKO Caine Prize rules of entry

The AKO Caine Prize is awarded annually to a short story by an African writer published in English, whether in Africa or elsewhere. The prize has become a benchmark for excellence in African writing.

An 'African writer' is taken to mean someone who was born in Africa, or who is a national of an African country, or who has a parent who is African by birth or nationality.

The indicative length is between 3,000 and 10,000 words.

There is a cash prize of £10,000 for the winning author, £500 for each shortlisted writer and a travel award for each of the shortlisted candidates (up to five in all).

For practical reasons, unpublished work and work in other languages is not eligible. Works translated into English from other languages are not excluded, provided they have been published in translation and, should such a work win, a proportion of the prize would be awarded to the translator.

The award is made in July each year, the deadline for submissions being 31 January. The shortlist is selected from work published in the five years preceding the submissions deadline and not previously considered for a Caine Prize. Submissions, including those from online journals, should be made by publishers and will need to be accompanied by six original published copies of the work for consideration, sent to the address below. There is no application form.

Every effort is made to publicize the work of the shortlisted authors through broadcast, online and printed media.

Winning and shortlisted authors will be invited to participate in writers' workshops in Africa and elsewhere as resources permit.

The above rules may be modified in the light of experience.

The AKO Caine Prize
Menier Chocolate Factory
51 Southwark Street
London, SE1 1RU, UK
Telephone: +44 (0)20 7378 6234
Email: info@caineprize.com
Website: caineprize.com
Find us on Facebook, Twitter @caineprize and Instagram.